# HUNGRY FOR THE WOLF

## GUARDED BY THE SHIFTER
### BOOK FOUR

## KATE RUDOLPH

Hungry for the Wolf © Kate Rudolph 2022.

All rights reserved. No part of this story may be used, reproduced or transmitted in any form or by any means without written permission of the copyright holder, except in the case of brief quotations embodied within critical reviews and articles.

This book is a work of fiction. The names, characters, places, and incidents are products of the writer's imagination or have been used fictitiously and are not to be construed as real. Any resemblance to persons, living or dead, actual events, locale or organizations is entirely coincidental.
Published by Kate Rudolph.
www.katerudolph.net

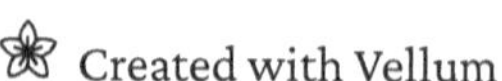 Created with Vellum

# ABOUT HUNGRY FOR THE WOLF

**Bryan has one job: keep Kerry safe.**

When Bryan's assigned to guard Kerry before she testifies in a high profile case, he expects it to be a simple job. Falling for her is against every rule, but no shifter can deny the mate bond.

**Kerry Delgado is anything but simple.**

When the bullets and fur start flying, Bryan discovers that he and Kerry have far more in common than he imagined. His wolf demands he does everything possible to keep her safe, but she's tangled up with dangerous men. And she may hold the key to the mystery of his pack's existence.

He's supposed to be a regular bodyguard, even if he's a werewolf. But when there's magic involved, nothing is simple. And if Bryan wants to claim Kerry as his own, he'll need to unravel the mystery before it's too late and he loses everything.

# CHAPTER ONE



No one was in the shop. Kerry flicked through a magazine, mostly looking at the pictures of sparkling celebrities and dapper suits, and tried not to wallow in her boredom. Everything was set up exactly as it should be, and it wasn't like the gallery normally had high traffic.

And none of her dad's people had been through in a week.

Thank god.

Air ruffled her hair as someone walked in. He was a white man in his forties, wearing a nice suit with no tie, and he had a haircut that probably cost close to a grand. She'd learned to spot rich marks when she was a baby, and though this guy was rich, he was no mark.

He didn't glance at the artwork on the wall, instead heading straight for her desk and pulling out a small business card and setting it on the table without a word.

He didn't *look* like one of her dad's clients. But numbers didn't lie.

"Well?" the man prompted when she didn't move fast enough.

Kerry was already in the process of standing, but was tempted to plunk her ass back down in the chair and make the man wait just a bit longer. She didn't have much power, but she could always annoy the guy.

But annoying rich guys with thousand-dollar haircuts never worked out well.

"Come with me," she said, palming the card and placing it into a locked drawer before leading the man towards the back of the gallery.

She could feel the eyes of one of the figures in a painting watching her as she led the man to the back. Watching and judging. And if Kerry were alone, she might tell the painting to mind its own business. But she didn't want the guy to think she was crazy.

It got lonely sitting in the gallery by herself all day, though. And sometimes the paintings felt like friends.

She opened the closet in the back and pulled out

the lone box that had been waiting for more than a week. That stupid box made her heart pound every time she heard a police siren outside. She didn't know what was in it and she'd never ask.

But her gallery funding had to come from somewhere. And she certainly wasn't selling enough paintings to afford Manhattan real estate.

A number scrawled in sharpie on a post-it note was the box's only label. Kerry took the post-it, careful not to otherwise touch the box, and nodded down at it. "That's what you came for."

The man stared at her. "Well, bring it along." He turned on a heel and started to walk away.

"I don't touch the boxes." Kerry kept her feet planted. "And you'll want to take this out the side door. No cameras." There wasn't an alley, of course. New York didn't really have alleys. But the side street was less busy and they wouldn't be observed.

The man stopped, turned back to her, and gave her a *look*. But he wasn't the first man to give her a hard look, and Kerry could more than handle herself. She gestured to the box and nodded towards the door.

They stared at one another for several long seconds until the man finally scowled and stalked over, scooping up the box as if it weighed nothing.

Kerry heard something rattle and hoped it wasn't fragile.

"Can you touch the door?" the man asked, voice dripping with contempt.

Kerry pasted on her best customer service smile, the only thing she'd learned from her one week working fashion retail, and led him towards the side door. She pushed it open and kicked the small brick into place to hold it wide while the man walked through.

There was a small park on the other side of the street, one she'd once imagined sitting in and eating her lunches. But scary men carrying numbered business cards could come in at any hour, and she'd never managed to leave the shop for long. She gave the park a longing look and startled when she thought she saw something big moving through the trees.

A coyote? A deer? A dog? She tried to look closer, but her client stomped out behind her and she lost sight of the animal.

He set the box down and pulled out his phone, typing something for a moment before slipping it back in his pocket. "My driver is circling the block."

She could leave him here, but something kept Kerry rooted in place. Her father wanted her to make sure the packages left the shop. And that meant ensuring the clients made it to their vehicles unscathed. Not that she could do much to stop a scathing, but that didn't mean she was allowed to retreat.

She'd done this a hundred times or more before. Nothing bad ever happened. And this guy would be no different.

But for some reason her heart was beating fast, and she wanted to go back inside. She had the strangest idea that once she was inside the store, she'd be safe. But the store was only marginally safer than the street. It wasn't like she could lock the front door. She still had a business to run.

The man let out a huff of frustration and she could almost relate. He probably never had to wait or carry his own shit. But he couldn't exactly control the stop lights his driver was sure to face.

There was a loud *pop* as a car backfired and Kerry jumped, eyes searching for the danger even as her brain tried to assure her all was well.

Tires screeched as two black cars met on the narrow street, and the man beside her cursed. One car rammed the other and Kerry's eyes went wide.

"What the hell?" For a second, it didn't occur to her that this was about the box. But the man was already running, box tucked under one arm as he raced to his car. A good Samaritan might call the cops to report the accident, but Kerry just wanted this day to end.

Then she heard another pop and realized it wasn't a car backfiring. Someone had a gun.

Kerry backed up and tried to get inside, but something had jostled the brick that kept the door open, and it was locked from the inside. Her focus narrowed as she crouched down, making herself as small as possible, and tried to figure out what was going on.

The man in the suit had run for his car and was taking cover behind it. He'd opened the box and was holding something and rocking back and forth. The car that had hit his had both doors open with two men standing and shooting like they were in the middle of an action movie. The driver was returning fire.

No one paid any attention to Kerry and she wanted it to stay that way. But if she stayed in place, her chances of getting hit by a stray bullet were good. And she didn't want to get shot. But running would only attract attention.

She scooted along the wall, trying to get to the dumpster just a bit further down. The smell would be godawful, but it was the only thing approaching real cover. And once she was out of sight, she could run.

She'd circle the building, lock the doors, and call her father to sort this shit out.

Her head pounded, and there was something just outside the scope of her senses, words she couldn't quite hear demanding to be let into her head. Kerry clamped her hands over her ears, but it did nothing to stop the intrusion. Neither did closing her eyes.

She didn't know how long she crouched, trying to block out something that didn't exist; it might have been a minute. Then her senses clued her in to an actual danger, something right in front of her she couldn't run from.

Wet, foul breath that punched her right in the face. A growl in the back of a throat. A monster.

Kerry forced her eyes open, sure this was some other illusion. She wasn't so lucky. She saw thick fur and yellow eyes. A dog, no, a *wolf*, bigger than any she'd seen, standing right in front of her and studying her like she was some sort of lab rat.

Somehow the chanting in her head got even louder. The wolf froze, and for a moment she had the crazy thought that it had turned to stone. But, no, it was still breathing, still waiting.

She couldn't run. The wolf was a predator and there were still gunshots. Why wasn't the wolf running from all of the noise?

Her concentration split for a second and the wolf lunged forward, clamping sharp teeth onto her arm, tearing at her skin and making her scream as white hot pain flashed through her.

Kerry fell as the wolf pulled her and she struggled against it. It was pulling her back towards the fight and she had no idea why. This was no normal wolf. They were in the middle of Manhattan. It couldn't be real.

The blood dripping down her wrist said otherwise.

She tried to push away the pain, but whoever said that was possible clearly had never been bitten by a wolf. But if she didn't do *something*, she was going to be forced into the middle of a gunfight, bleeding, and unsure of what was going on.

She reached out, hand scrambling for anything she could use as a weapon. They weren't far from the dumpster and her fingers closed around the edge of a glass beer bottle.

Kerry pulled back against the wolf, even as she expected it to dig in and tear her arm off. But there was something almost gentle about it. She was hurt, bleeding, and probably needed stitches, but she had the idea that a wolf could do a lot more damage than this one.

So why wasn't it?

No time to wonder.

She swung the bottle and smashed it against the wolf's snout. It let go.

Kerry burst to her feet, an impossible explosion of adrenaline giving her speed. Any thought of not running from a predator was obliterated by her fear. She clutched her bleeding arm to her chest and rounded the corner, screaming for help and hoping someone would hear her.

The gunshots had faded, but she only distantly noticed that.

Red and blue lights flashed, a cop car coming to a stop so close to her that she almost ran into it. The officers were out in a blink, guns drawn and pointed at her.

"On the ground!" they demanded, as if she wasn't crying, bleeding, and running for her life.

Kerry collapsed. At least she didn't see the wolf anymore.

# CHAPTER TWO

**Present Day**

Bryan Vega stalked his prey. They were in the woods behind the farm and he'd caught the scent only a minute ago. He wasn't in his wolf skin, not today. It made stalking all the more difficult.

And that much more fun.

He stepped carefully, not letting leaves crunch under his boots. His prey didn't know he was only a few steps away, and he intended to keep it that way. As long as the wind didn't shift, he had this.

It ruffled the leaves on the trees and he tipped his head back, enjoying the breeze. Fall was his favorite time of year, and it was only starting to cool off. Soon enough they'd be huddled around a fire and making s'mores.

But not tonight. Tonight, he was a hunter. And a winner.

He surged forward, tackling the blonde woman to the ground and flashing his teeth at her.

Stasia's eyes went wide and her hands went up to ward him off.

Bryan froze as another scene flashed through his mind.

*Pain. Bright light. A demanding feminine voice. The slice of a scalpel.*

*Heat.*

*The shift.*

*Blood.*

He reared back and slid off Stasia, hands and knees on the ground as the memory threatened to make him puke. The wind teased his nose with another scent as Owen Myers, Stasia's mate, found them.

"Which one of you won?" he asked with a damned smile in his voice. The man was way too cheerful. Somehow the Army had never beaten it out of him, never mind he'd been in for nearly a decade longer than Bryan.

"I'm the one standing," Stasia said, her voice cool and sharp. She was all hard edges and seriousness next to Owen, and their relationship still made no sense to Bryan, but he didn't have a right to question it.

After all, he'd almost killed her.

"I got you." He forced himself to stand and breathe through his mouth as if he wasn't in the middle of a low grade freak out. It had been nearly a year. Stasia was healthy, happy, and completely fine. No permanent damage.

If she was over it, why couldn't he do the same?

Stasia and Owen were both looking at him like they were afraid he was going to collapse like a nineteenth century maiden suffering from the vapors. Bryan fixed a scowl onto his face and flipped them both off.

Owen cackled and Stasia rolled her eyes.

"From what I saw, my lovely mate was the clear victor," Owen declared, slinging his arm around Stasia and leading them both towards the edge of the woods.

"You'd say that no matter what," Bryan muttered. "That's why you're not in charge of deciding the winner."

"There are no winners." Stasia glanced back at him, cool eyes sympathetic. She didn't offer him pity, didn't try and forgive him again for what he'd done to her. She knew he didn't need to hear it. "This was a training exercise. And I *do* need to get better at not letting people sneak up on me."

Owen grinned. "But you like it when I sneak up on you."

Was that a *blush* from the pack doctor? There was a story there, and if she'd been anyone else, Bryan would have let his tongue fly. Instead, teasing words got locked up in the back of his throat and he nearly choked on them.

They entered through the basement of the house. It was a big farmhouse that led out onto acres of open land and forest, perfect for the weirdest werewolf, no, *shifter,* pack in existence. Apparently, werewolves didn't like to be called werewolves.

Weird.

"Where's Jackson?" Owen asked as he slipped out of his leather jacket and hung it on a hook by the door. "I swear she was here." He breathed in deep.

Bryan tested the scents in the air and might have caught a whiff of their packmate, but he wasn't sure. They all spent so much time at the farm that their scents were embedded in the walls. "I didn't see her," he said.

"She came by earlier to speak to Jericho," Stasia answered.

"Jericho?" Owen's face screwed up in horror. "You're calling him *that?*"

"It is his name, dear." The sarcasm dripped from her words, but Bryan didn't know if Owen was even capable of picking it up.

"Vega, up here," the man in question, Major Jericho Gibson, called down the stairs.

Bryan and Owen both froze as if they'd been caught in a tractor beam while Stasia continued to look at them like they were idiots. Bryan shook himself out of it after a moment and waved goodbye to his companions, his momentary lapse in the woods forgotten.

Gibson was waiting in the small room he'd designated as an office. It wasn't quite big enough to be called a bedroom, though there was a rolled up cot under Gibson's desk in case of emergencies. Luckily, the house normally had more than enough spaces for people to sleep.

But their pack was growing. First Stasia had joined them, then her sister Em. Now Vi, who was a freaking *witch,* like that was something that existed.

Big words coming from a werewolf.

No, *shifter.*

The thoughts rushed by in Bryan's head quickly

enough that Gibson didn't catch him daydreaming. Good. He'd disappointed the boss enough already.

Gibson nodded at the seat opposite his small desk. He was shoved in behind it and looked a bit like a sausage with a casing that was about to burst. The room was too small for him. It wasn't that Gibson was a huge man, but he had a presence. It filled up every square inch of the room and demanded more.

Bryan was pretty sure that *he* couldn't fill up even one corner of this glorified closet.

He heard footsteps outside the office as Owen and Stasia came upstairs and headed for the kitchen.

"I've received a request from a friend and I want you to take the assignment." Gibson slid a small stack of paper towards him. The first page was a news article about a shooting in Manhattan from a year before. Under that he spotted a file of a woman; her picture was in black and white and looked as if it had been photocopied more than once. He couldn't make out much about her.

"She was shot?" Bryan scanned the article but didn't waste time reading it in front of the boss. He'd do that later.

Gibson shook his head. "Witnessed a shooting. She manages an art gallery, customer came in, went out the back, a gunfight ensued. She saw the whole thing. At least, she's the only one willing to talk. But the prosecutor is afraid someone might stop her from making it to the stand."

"The gunman?" Bryan's shoulder ached in memory of the worst bullet wound he'd ever suffered.

"Not sure. Not our problem. Apparently the gallery has connections to organized crime, and Ms. Delgado, your charge, is the daughter of a man who's been connected to more than one mob hit in the last decade. Not the trigger man, of course. He's too high up for that." Gibson scowled, though Bryan didn't know if it was a general reaction to crime or something about this man in particular. "I briefly served with the lead detective on the case. He asked if I could send someone to watch over the witness for the next couple of weeks."

"Have there been any attempts on the witness? Or are we being extra cautious?" Bryan flicked his thumb against the edge of the pages, knowing they might hold the answer. But reading could wait.

"A different young woman was mugged a block from Ms. Delgado's apartment. Could be a coincidence, but they are roughly the same height and have similar hair colors. The mugger demanded a wallet and when he read the victim's ID, he threw it on the ground and ran, as if he had the wrong person. You're to be Ms. Delgado's shadow. Is that clear?" Gibson looked at him as if he had all the faith in the world that he could do this.

Bryan wasn't sure. He hadn't flown solo since the shooting, and only rarely before then. But Gibson wouldn't give him the assignment if he wasn't confident in his abilities.

"I'm free," Owen said from the doorway. He leaned against the frame, a casual smile on his face. "I'd be happy to spot him."

Gibson leveled his gaze at Owen. "So you've discovered the owner of the phone number you're investigating and determined whether or not Dr. Nichols' brother has anything to do with our transformation or the disappearances we learned about a few months ago?"

Owen gulped and his smile slipped. "We're still working on it. Stasia's brother is a hard guy to pin down."

"Undoubtedly." Gibson laced his fingers together. "You're on standby, but I want Vega solo on this. Only come if he calls. He doesn't need a babysitter. Got it?"

Owen nodded quickly. "Yes, sir."

Bryan clutched the papers in his hands and hoped he was worthy of the faith Gibson was putting in him.

# CHAPTER THREE

Cutting through the park cut twenty minutes off Kerry's subway ride home. She'd been doing it for years and never had any trouble. Sure, sometimes there were creeps, but that was part of the charm of living in the city.

The guys behind her were more than creeps.

Sweat beaded on Kerry's brow and she quickened her pace. The path winded through a bunch of trees that looked beautiful on a sunny day. On an overcast one like today with the sun threatening to disappear at any moment, they held only foreboding.

No. That was her imagination getting the best of her. The guys behind her were just men. They probably didn't even realize they were freaking her out. This was her own brain playing tricks on her.

She walked a little faster.

The walk through the park took ten minutes and she was only just past the entrance. But the path would split up ahead, and hopefully the men behind her would go a different way.

Of course, she wasn't that lucky.

"Hey there, pretty lady!" one of them called from behind. They were closer than she thought. Had they jogged to catch up?

She was pretty sure there were three of them and she wished she had a weapon, a taser or pepper spray or something that would send them running.

*You do have a weapon*, a dark and twisted voice whispered inside of her.

But she wasn't thinking about *that* at the moment.

Something felt like it was moving under her skin, demanding to be let out, and Kerry clamped down on that instinct before it led to bloodshed. The worst these guys could do to her was steal her purse. She liked her purse, but not enough to kill for it.

She wouldn't let them do anything else.

She stopped before the path led them even deeper into the wooded area. Out here someone might see them, might hear her scream. She didn't want to give away that advantage.

When she turned, her instincts were confirmed.

Three men, young, white, wearing baggy clothes they probably thought made them look tough. Or bigger. They were skinny. How old could they be? Eighteen?

But the hate and desire on their faces was real, and it sent fear shivering down her spine.

*You don't have to be afraid anymore*, that dark voice whispered.

*Shut up*, Kerry snapped back. She was the one in charge.

Dear God, hopefully ADA Michaels never heard Kerry argue with herself like that. She'd be off the witness stand so fast there'd be scorch marks. Laughter threatened to bubble up at the thought and Kerry was tempted to let it out.

That would freak these guys out.

"You're cute," the second scrawny man told her. "We could show you a good time."

"Leave me alone." The urge to run beat hard inside of her. These skinny little boys shouldn't have been any threat. They were an annoyance at best. But angry boys like these could do a lot of damage. And at least Kerry was strong enough to take it. She'd hate to think of what would happen if they cornered someone else.

The third one broke formation and took a step towards her. He lifted his hand, as if he was going to curl it in her hair, but he wasn't quite close enough.

Still, Kerry jerked back. His smile was slimy and made her skin crawl. "Come on," he cajoled. "You're just our type. Pretty, pretty redhead. Is it natural?" His eyes flicked down to her crotch.

"Gross!" Kerry stumbled back. Did the creep really just ask that? Out loud? "What the fuck? Get out of here!" She wasn't screaming. Not yet. But hopefully her resistance would be enough to discourage these boys.

The first and second creeps stepped up beside the third, and the first one was close enough that he was able to touch her hair. "Soft," he said. Spittle flicked on his lips.

Violence bubbled in Kerry's veins and she wanted to give these boys a lesson. But it rode her so hard that she forced herself to quell it. She wasn't a violent person. Or she hadn't been. Before. And if she let the full breadth of her rage out on these creeps, she'd kill them.

She'd seen enough violence to last a lifetime already.

Several lifetimes.

"Not interested." She swatted their hands away. "Walk away and leave me, and every other woman in this park, alone." Her dad had a way of speaking that made men rush to obey before he could even ask.

Unfortunately that gene hadn't been passed down. Maybe it was a guy thing.

"Lighten up," the first guy said, and she had a feeling he was the ringleader. "We just want to have a bit of fun. We're giving you a compliment."

"Leave me alone," she repeated. And she hated that she heard trembling in her voice. Blood rushed in her ears, and she feared she wouldn't be able to hold off the violence for much longer.

"This bitch needs to learn how to have fun," the second guy sneered and reached into his pocket. He came back with a knife. "We're all gonna walk nice and quiet over there," he nodded to a copse of trees off the path, "and you're not gonna say a word, girlie. Got it?"

Kerry looked at the knife, then her eyes flicked up to him. His hand didn't tremble, but he was holding on tight to his little piece of external masculinity. The blade was wickedly sharp and could do some damage.

"Have you ever used it?" she asked, the darkness inside of her pulsing through her veins and threatening to burst out of her skin.

The guy's grip tightened even more and she heard him swallow. "Do what I said, bitch!" He waved the knife wildly. "Do it or I use *this*. Take her purse, Greg," he demanded.

*When it comes to violence, just do it. Don't threaten. Threats are a weakness. Do what must be done and walk away.*

That voice wasn't her own darkness. Her father wasn't there to protect her, but she'd learned her lessons well. And before the boy with the knife could anticipate it, her hand darted out and grabbed his wrist before she headbutted him like she was some kind of UFC champion.

It all went by in a blur after that, but thirty seconds later, the scrawny boys were running home with their tails tucked between their legs, and her purse was still slung over her shoulder. Her forehead burned and her so did her eye. One of the boys had gotten a punch in before she grabbed onto his wrist and heard a sickening crack.

She wondered how long her eye would take to heal. Would she even see the bruises once she was home?

Kerry walked out of the park with confidence in her step, and no one dared to bother her, not that they usually did. But today she felt dangerous. Victorious.

*As you should.*

And the voice in her head didn't feel as dark. It was more a part of her than ever. A year ago, she would have run screaming in fear from that fight.

But she didn't have to be afraid anymore.

Kerry let herself into her apartment building and trudged up the stairs. It smelled faintly of the sandwiches from the bodega downstairs and from whatever delicious concoctions they were cooking up at the Asian-Mexican fusion place next door. Her stomach growled.

Yeah, definitely time to eat.

Something tickled her nose when she got to her own door on the third floor, and Kerry paused. She looked at the door across the hall and wondered if her neighbor had a guest. Or maybe it had been a delivery guy.

Her nose was going into overdrive. There was no way to understand it all in Manhattan and she'd figured out how to ignore most scents to stop herself from going crazy.

So why did this one give her pause?

Kerry pushed it out of her mind. She was home. She was safe. She could deal with it later.

But as she pushed the door open, she realized her mistake.

There was a man sitting at her kitchen counter. Her adrenaline was on overload and she acted before she could think, chucking her purse at him and charging forward with a scream.

# CHAPTER FOUR

Bryan realized his mistake as the redhead charged at him, her purse missing him by a mile and clattering to the floor. Sure, Gibson might have given him a key to her apartment, one he'd somehow gotten off of his cop friend, but that didn't mean that Bryan should have let himself in.

Really, he was an idiot. And this mission was about to fail before it ever began.

He threw his hands up in surrender. "I'm here to help, I swear. I'm sorry for letting myself in." His wolf grumbled under his skin at the way he surrendered before the fight even began, but he wasn't going to *fight* the woman he was charged to protect.

She skidded to a halt and glared at him.

Fury blazed bright, and with the red hair falling in

waves, she looked like an ancient goddess, the kind that walked through battlefields naked and slayed everyone who dared to look at her.

Bryan could do with seeing a little more. She was gorgeous. The thought, and the desire that followed it, slammed into him, and a tiny part of him wished she'd kept charging so long as it meant he got to feel her pressed up against him.

And then he noticed the darkening, swollen skin around her eye and his stomach roiled. He was off the bench and striding towards her before his judgement could think better of it.

She flinched.

Bryan stopped, hand raised halfway between them. "Who did this to you?" He'd hunt them down and destroy them for daring to lay a hand on his charge. His wolf growled and threatened to burst out of him, but Bryan clamped down on his control. No way was he about to go wolfy ten seconds after he was caught breaking into this goddess's apartment.

He didn't want to scare her.

Not again.

Ms. Delgado raised her hand to her cheek and lightly brushed the skin. Strangely, she smiled as she winced. "You should see the other guys."

"*Guys?*" He'd already failed the mission. Day zero

and she was sporting a black eye and fighting her own battles.

Battles and bruises were supposed to be his job.

"It's not as bad as it looks," she assured him. "It'll be gone before long. I don't bruise easily." She backed up and raised a hand to lock her door before looking at him again and leaving it unlocked. "Tell me why you're here and then get out. And tell me how you got in." There was steel in her voice. Steel and fire.

Bryan slowly reached into his pocket and pulled out a business card. He held it out to her. "My name is Bryan Vega. I'm a bodyguard. That's my company's information. The lead detective on your case was concerned for your safety and called in a favor with my boss. I'm here to make sure nothing—nothing *else*—happens to you before you testify."

She snatched the card out of his hand and studied it as if it held the secrets of the universe. Once she'd confirmed it didn't, she set it down on her small kitchen table. "That's why you're here. How did you get in?"

"The detective had a key." He pulled that out of his pocket as well and handed it over. "He said there was some trouble here a few years ago and your super gave the keys over."

Ms. Delgado took the key as well and glared at it.

If she had laser eyes it would have been melted already. And, frankly, Bryan wouldn't be surprised if she managed to melt them anyway just with the fury of her gaze. "I didn't know there'd been trouble. Or that he had my key. Must have been before I moved in."

He'd have to have words with the detective to make sure there were no other keys floating around out there. If Ms. Delgado didn't kick him out.

She made a curious sound. "Detective Rawlins sent you. Not my father?"

"His name was Detective Harper." And Bryan had talked to him for nearly half an hour. He'd never heard of Rawlins. And when Ms. Delgado nodded, he realized he'd passed a test. "I don't know your father," he said. "He didn't send me and I'm not following his orders. I just want to keep you safe in case anyone is coming for you."

"My father might offer you a lot of money," she said, and he couldn't tell if it was a warning.

"I wish I could tell you that I'm a billionaire only masquerading as a bodyguard. I'm not. But I'm not so strapped for cash that I'd betray a client. Sounds like things might be tense with your dad, so he doesn't get close." He wasn't exactly sure how he would keep a mob boss out of their hair, but that was a problem for later. And, luckily, as far as he knew, her father wasn't the one threatening her.

"What do you know about the threats?" She was still standing in front of the door and clutching her apartment key.

He wished there was an easy way to put her at ease, but all Bryan could give her was the truth. "There was a mugging of a woman near here. She resembled you, and her mugger ran after looking at her identification. And there have been a few break ins in the area, though those could be normal property crime. No one was home, and electronics and some cash were stolen. As for why, you're a witness to a violent crime."

"What do you know about that?" she prompted. Her whole body was strung as tight as a bow string.

He wanted to wrap his arms around her and promise that nothing bad would ever happen to her. He wanted to run his lips over the fine skin of her neck and taste every inch of her. He wanted more than he'd ever dared dream and he didn't understand it.

He had to get control of himself.

"I read an article about the shooting, you weren't named. Detective Harper wouldn't tell me much more. If it doesn't directly impact my job, I don't need to know." Sure, he was curious. He had a mind that liked to solve puzzles. But right now, the puzzle he was trying to solve was Kerry Delgado. "Obviously the prosecutors want you on that stand. It's my job to see you get there."

"ADA Michaels did say something about calling in security," she said, mostly to herself.

Bryan had never spoken with the ADA but decided not to offer that. Ms. Delgado was on the verge of accepting him. He stared at her while she thought.

And he noticed the redness under her eye *had* faded. She was right about not bruising easily. Though he still wanted to take her pain away.

Ms. Delgado gave a tight nod. "Fine. You can stay. But don't get in my way."

"I won't, Ms. Delgado." Something about her name didn't taste right on his tongue, but Bryan was determined to be professional. Gibson had put his faith in him and Bryan wouldn't mess it up.

"Please, call me Kerry."

Kerry it was.

# CHAPTER FIVE

They'd barely had a moment to get settled in before Kerry's phone started ringing, the shrill alarm loud enough to make Bryan wince. Kerry scrambled for her phone, fishing it out of her fallen purse and answering with a breathless word.

Something must have been off with her speaker; Bryan could barely make out the conversation, and ever since he'd been changed into a werewolf his senses had heightened a bit. He should have been able to hear. But he was just the bodyguard. He wasn't welcome in Kerry's private conversations.

Kerry.

He liked the way her name felt and he formed it silently while she spoke. He'd spent the last day while he prepared for this job forcing himself to think of her as Ms. Delgado, his client, even though everything within him protested at the thought.

Kerry.

Yes, that was much better. And if he wanted to whisper it to her while he drove himself inside of her and brought her to the heights of pleasure, *that* was something he'd keep to himself. This was a job and he was here to be professional.

He wouldn't fuck up.

His body still hadn't gotten the message. But Bryan wasn't completely ruled by lust, and he managed to calm himself down mostly by the time Kerry finished her call and scowled at her phone.

"Is there a problem?" he asked. He'd hoped they could stay in the apartment and get to know one another. He even had a coupon for a nearby pizza place to sweeten the deal. But from the way Kerry was scooping up her purse and shoving things back inside, staying in wasn't an option.

"That was ADA Michaels. She needs me to stop by her office *now*. Apparently the entire case will fall apart if we're not across town and sitting in front of her desk in the next three minutes." She straightened and hooked her bag over her shoulder.

"I can't teleport, sorry." If he could, he would have

immediately revealed that power. It was easier to keep the whole werewolf thing a secret.

"Then I guess we'll have to take the subway." She led the way back out of the apartment and gave him a pointed look as she locked up behind them.

Bryan didn't try to bite back his smile. Kerry had spirit, and a tough year hadn't beaten it out of her. He wanted to see more.

"What does she need you to do?" he asked once they'd boarded the subway. There were only a few other people in the car, luckily. If the prosecutor had called an hour later, they would have been packed in like sardines. "I'm not really sure how court actually works." But he had binge watched four seasons of *The Good Wife* a few years back. That had to count for something.

"There's paperwork and statements and practice trials and a ton I never realized was involved. I guess a lot of cases don't actually get this far. Most people take plea deals to avoid longer sentences. ADA Michaels really wants to nail this guy. And apparently one misplaced piece of paperwork could destroy it all." She rolled her eyes and swayed as the train turned a corner.

Bryan kept his awareness on the other passengers in the car and noted when they left or someone new entered. If he had his way, he'd be leading his charge through the city in an armored vehicle and running over any threat before they could think about doing anything.

But this was New York and the subway was their best option.

Afternoon was edging towards evening by the time they made it up the steps outside the ADA's office, and the streets were starting to fill with people heading home. The ride back would be much more crowded and Bryan would have to be on high alert.

He kept his senses open as they entered the building. It looked just like any other office building, but Bryan still had the nagging sense that one of the detectives from *Law and Order* would tackle him if he made one wrong move.

He was here as a bodyguard, he couldn't be jumpy like that. Not if he was going to keep Kerry safe.

They walked up the stairs and he kept looking for threats. Though he'd spotted a security guard downstairs and saw cameras on every landing of the staircase, this building would still be a target if someone wanted to take Kerry out. Here or right outside. All her assailants would need were eyes inside the building.

Not that there were any assailants. He couldn't jump to conclusions, otherwise he'd be jumping the first suspicious person to cross his path. He could see the headlines now: *Crazed Vet Attacks Old Lady.*

Or even worse: *Crazed Vet Turns into Wolf, Attacks Old Lady.*

Yeah, not what he needed.

Kerry nudged his shoulder and he startled. "Are you paying attention?" she demanded.

He grimaced and tried to cover it. "Always aware of our surroundings."

She snorted, clearly not buying it. "We're here."

They gave their names to a receptionist and he had to let Kerry go once a tall woman in a business suit with dark skin and long black braids led her back. ADA Michaels. The woman barely spared Bryan a glance, but he was satisfied that Kerry would be safe so long as she was in the office.

Bryan sat in the hallway outside the prosecutor's office and let his senses wander, but not his mind. He was keeping himself open to anything that didn't belong, even if he severely doubted that anyone would actually get to the prosecutor's office to cause trouble.

No, the trouble would be outside.

But something tickled his nose and Bryan stood, trying to investigate the instinct. He heard footsteps and walked towards the stairs, seeing a man walk down a hallway one floor below.

Bryan looked at the door to the office and then back downstairs.

He had to check this out. And now he wished that Owen was there with him. This really was a team job. But if someone was setting up an ambush, it was better that he ran into it rather than Kerry.

Bryan rushed down the stairs and spotted the man turn another corner. There was something off about his scent, but Bryan couldn't name it. His senses were enhanced, but they weren't supernaturally good unless he was wearing his other skin. And he wasn't crazy enough to transform into a wolf in an office building in midtown.

The second hallway was dimmer than the last, the fluorescent light overhead flickering and on the verge of death, but Bryan could still see.

Well enough that he saw a side door clang shut and the security panel next to it beep before resetting. The hallway ended a few paces later. The man had disappeared.

Not disappeared. He'd gone into a secure room.

Bryan looked for a sign on the door, but there was no indication of who it belonged to. And the keypad looked formidable, but he'd seen similar models in other offices. It wasn't anything special.

He tested the door anyway, hoping it was magically unlocked, though he didn't know what he planned to do if it did open.

It didn't.

He stared at the door for several minutes, but the man didn't come back out. And Bryan had to give up. His job was to protect Kerry, not chase strangers. But it was hard to walk away when his instincts were pounding at him, insisting something was wrong.

He'd get back to the office and find Kerry, and everything would be fine. It had to be.

And that thought lasted until the moment a security guard stepped in front of him, taser clutched in both hands and pointing straight at him.

# CHAPTER SIX

The guest chair in ADA Michaels' office wasn't comfortable. Kerry had noticed that the first time she'd sat there and relayed the story of the shooting. By their fifth meeting, she'd grown to truly loath the chair, with its spring poking into her butt and the fabric cracking around the edges, so much that she was tempted to chuck it out the window and blame it on an intern.

But the interns hadn't done anything wrong and Kerry *really* didn't want to get on ADA Michaels' bad side. The woman was formidable.

Kerry read through the documents she'd needed to rush over to sign and scrawled her name where little brightly colored tabs indicated she was supposed to. "I could have sworn I've signed this form before," she said as she finished writing the date.

Michaels leaned back in her chair and glared down at it when it squeaked. The guest chair wasn't the only one with issues. "You may have. Some papers were misfiled and we need to get this cleared up before the defense attorney pounces on it."

Once the final document was signed, Kerry pushed them back towards Michaels. "All done. Anything else?"

"Yeah. Michaels glanced at the closed door behind her as if she could see through it. "The receptionist said you came in with a man. Who's that?"

A tiny bit of alarm wiggled its way into Kerry's mind. "His name is Bryan Vega. He's a bodyguard. He said Harper sent him. He made it sound like you'd cleared it." Hadn't he? Kerry's mind had still been reeling from the fight and she hadn't been on top of her game. Especially with the added adrenaline rush from seeing a stranger in her home. "You did clear it, right?"

Michaels picked up the receiver on her desk and pressed a button. "Have security ready." She put the phone back down.

The alarm grew. "Ms. Michaels..."

"I've never heard of Bryan Vega. I haven't okayed

any security for you, and Detective Harper hasn't said a word about it. Tell me exactly how he showed up."

Kerry straightened in her seat at the command. In another life, Michaels would have made an excellent drill instructor. And so she laid it all out, not that there was much to tell. She'd only known Vega for two hours.

But something inside of her protested the idea that he might be there to cause her harm. He wouldn't.

She couldn't know that.

*He wouldn't.*

It was the dark voice of her other self. The one she tried to pretend didn't exist at moments like these. Kerry had never been one to blindly follow her instincts, but in the last year those instincts had driven her nearly mad.

And now here they were trying to tell her that some stranger was a friend.

Michaels stood up once Kerry was done with the stories. "Stay here," she warned. "I want to talk with your new friend. And call Harper. We need to sort this out."

She left Kerry in the room alone. Kerry slumped back in her uncomfortable chair and wished she could start this day over. Maybe if she refused to get out of bed, nothing would go wrong.

It hadn't worked yet, but one of these days, maybe a genie would show up to grant her three wishes.

Yeah, right. Kerry'd had enough of mythical creatures.

Her arm throbbed and she rubbed it, the pain no more real than her imagined genie. She nearly jumped out of her seat when her phone buzzed. She reached into her bag and glared at the caller information.

Dad.

Ugh.

She could ignore it. But he'd just call back. Eventually. And the more she ignored him, the more he'd resent it. And a resentful father led to even worse calls.

She accepted the call. And a moment later she already regretted it.

———

The security guard kept back a few steps and ushered Bryan to a small room down the hall from the prosecutor's office. Bryan kept his hands up and didn't try and explain himself. The guard looked jumpy and didn't have any real power.

No, this was the doing of ADA Michaels.

For some reason.

For a moment he wondered if she was working against Kerry, if she had something to do with the mugging or the possible threats to his charge. He dismissed the thought almost as quickly. The ADA needed Kerry, and she wanted the big win this case would give her.

"Sit." The guard nodded towards a single, spindly, wooden chair in the corner of what had to be the security office. There were two large computer screens on an old steel desk and the screens showed security camera footage from around the building. Bryan did his best to sneak a peek, but he only caught a glimpse of pictures that his mind didn't have time to make sense of.

Oh well.

He sat quietly.

Gibson would kill him if something went wrong. No. Gibson would be *disappointed* in him, which was even worse. Bryan had led his whole life quietly and not-so-quietly disappointing everyone around him. His parents hadn't been surprised when his military career was suddenly cut short. And they'd run out of any true ability to care when he was in high school.

Perfect older siblings would do that to a kid.

He shoved the thought of his siblings out of his

mind. He didn't care what they were doing, and they had no effect on his life. This was his job and he was going to do it. Whatever bug the ADA had up her ass, he'd extract it... or however you were supposed to deal with a bug up the ass situation.

He shook his head before he could follow that line of reasoning any farther.

"You need to clear this shit with me before you make these calls. I almost had that boy arrested." He heard the words coming from down the hallway. The security guard didn't react, so it must have been out of the range of human hearing.

Good thing Bryan wasn't exactly human anymore.

"No, Harper, this isn't your call. Your call would involve putting officers outside her house. Not hiring out. Why?" She paused for a second to let the cop talk. Whatever he said must have ended the call.

By the time ADA Michaels made it to the security office, she'd buried all the frustration she'd vented on the detective and looked almost serene. "I apologize for the misunderstanding, Mr. Vega. Detective Harper had not yet notified me that you'd been hired."

Why would he? Luckily Bryan held the question back. He didn't want to be on the other side of a death glare from this woman. But he wondered if there was more to this case than he understood. "I see. No hard feelings. Where is Ms. Delgado?" He could be professional. His only job was to keep Kerry safe, and while he had little doubt she'd be protected in the prosecutor's office, he wanted to see for himself.

He wasn't going to screw this job up.

"She was just finishing up and is still in my office. Let's go collect her and then you can be on your way."

It sounded perfect. And they could still use that pizza coupon. Bryan's stomach was already starting to growl, ready for dinner.

But when they got back to the ADA's office, Kerry was gone.

# CHAPTER SEVEN

Bryan rushed out of the office with barely a farewell to Michaels. The receptionist let him know that Kerry had left ten minutes before him. Not much lead time, but enough that chasing her through the city would be impossible.

He wanted to curse out Michaels for making Kerry doubt him. But that would have to wait until he had Kerry safe once more.

If he'd been on the job a little longer and had Kerry's consent, he'd be able to track her phone. But they'd rushed out of the apartment before he could talk about setting that up. It would be the first thing he did once he found her.

And there weren't many places she was likely to go.

Bryan headed back to her place, anxiety pounding in him every second of the ride back. He should have never let her out of his sight. If he'd gone into the ADA's office with her, he could have explained himself and never had to deal with this misunderstanding.

There was no use wishing he could change the past. His limited supernatural abilities didn't extend that far and though he and his pack were discovering new things about themselves all the time, no one had revealed time travel powers.

Yet.

He'd have to ask Vi about it. The witch, Rowe's mate, knew a million times more things about the supernatural than he did. She'd been teaching them what she could, but she and Rowe were investigating treachery that had torn Vi's coven apart, and she only had so much time for Remedial Werewolf School.

Once Bryan made it to Kerry's building, he scanned the surrounding area for threats. So far there wasn't anything out of the ordinary. But this was New York and *ordinary* had its own kind of weirdness.

He just needed to find Kerry and explain things. This didn't have to be a big deal.

The trudge up the stairs felt longer than it should have and Bryan dreaded what Kerry would say once he found her. Was her trust completely broken? Or would she accept there had just been a misunderstanding?

He regretted giving up her apartment key. But he dismissed that thought as soon as it came. The trust between them would be utterly destroyed if he was stupid enough to let himself in without her permission another time.

Bryan heard footsteps in the stairway and listened for anything threatening. But this *was* a regular apartment building with plenty of other tenants. The footsteps faded as the person moved further away. No threat.

He knocked on Kerry's door.

No answer.

For a moment Bryan wondered if he'd made the wrong guess and Kerry hadn't gone home. Perhaps she'd sought shelter with her father. That would be a safe place, so long as he wasn't the one threatening her in the first place. There was no indication that he was involved, but Bryan couldn't exactly dismiss his threat. He was a mob boss, after all.

But any doubts went away when he heard footsteps in Kerry's apartment and her voice coming through the door. "Go away or I'll call the cops."

He held back a sigh. Not good. "I'm here to help you, Kerry." He couldn't leave, and the cops would complicate things. He didn't know how Detective Harper would react to Kerry calling officers on him.

"You lied to me," she accused.

Had he? Bryan tried to recall all of the details of their first conversation. If he'd lied, it had been on accident or by omission. It wasn't like he was going to tell her he could shift into a wolf and howl at the moon. Not on the first date.

His mind quickly summoned up things he *could* do with her on a first date, and Bryan had to clamp down on that before this conversation went any more sideways.

"I didn't," he insisted. "I really am here as a favor to Detective Harper. ADA Michaels called him and sorted this out. He hadn't cleared it with her before calling me in. That's all. I'm exactly who I said I am."

There were more footsteps in the hall and Bryan wondered if they were starting to get onlookers. This probably looked like a lovers' quarrel. But Bryan wasn't Kerry's lover yet.

At all. Damn it. He had to keep this professional.

"Promise me you're telling the truth." She sounded like she was begging for a lifeline.

Something squeezed Bryan's heart, and he wanted to reach through the door and gather Kerry into his arms and hold her close until all her doubts melted away. But he couldn't give her that.

So he gave her what he could. "I promise."

He heard the lock disengage, and the door opened. Kerry's eyes were red and she looked as if she'd been crying. Bryan's heart ached, but he pushed that thought aside. He might have only known Kerry for a couple hours, but he was almost certain she wouldn't want to talk about it. Especially not in the open.

"It really was just a misunderstanding," he promised. "I'm here to keep you safe."

She nodded and backed up to let him into the apartment. Footsteps pounded up the steps behind him and Bryan glanced back.

The man he'd spotted at the prosecutor's office was on the landing below, a dark object in his hand. Bryan registered what it was just as a bullet dug into the frame of Kerry's apartment door.

Bryan dived inside and slammed the door shut behind him.

# CHAPTER EIGHT

Kerry heard the gunshot at the same moment Bryan dived into the apartment and slammed the door. And for a heartrending second, she thought he'd been hit, that she'd have this man bleeding out on her floor while someone laid siege to her hallway.

But Bryan sprang up, eyes bright and a little... strange. He pointed at her. "Call the police." Was his voice deeper?

Her mind was playing tricks on her. And his command was enough to jolt her out of her frozen state and have her reaching for her phone. She could curse her father for his call now. He'd fucked with her head, just like he always did, and that, far more than the doubts that ADA Michaels had raised, had sent Kerry running back home.

The police. Right.

Kerry couldn't dwell on her dad, not right now. She unlocked her phone and tried to dial, but the call wouldn't go through. "I don't have a signal." Which was weird. The reception in her apartment was usually really good.

Bryan didn't waste time doubting her. "Landline?" he asked.

She shook her head. "Never bothered." It hadn't seemed like a big deal at the time. Who had a landline anymore?

More shots tore into the door and Kerry shrank back into the apartment.

Bryan reached into his pocket and tossed something at her. His phone. She fumbled the catch, but didn't drop it. She didn't need to be told what to do. She didn't need his pass code to dial 911, but it didn't matter. "Still no signal."

Bryan cursed and took his phone back. "He might have a signal jammer. Get back." He looked around her room, utterly calm. Kerry was ready to explode with tension and he looked like he was reading through the menu at Panera. What the hell?

Kerry got back, and flinched at every bullet, but there were only two more before he stopped. "What are the chances someone else calls the cops?"

Her bodyguard didn't look back at her while he answered. "Low if he's using a signal jammer. It could easily block all calls from the building. Is there a fire escape?"

"No." The building wasn't old enough to need one. It had seemed like a good thing when Kerry found the apartment. Now she was cursing her luck. "He's stopped shooting. Do you think he's run out of bullets?" Maybe she was being too hopeful.

Almost certainly too hopeful.

"He's waiting. Shooting the door isn't working, but he has us pinned." Bryan let out a string of profanity that might have made her blush in other circumstances. "If I had a gun, things would be different."

Kerry swallowed hard. "I have a gun." Her hands had started shaking every time she took it for target practice, but it was in her apartment.

"Get it." Bryan approached the door and Kerry wanted to call him back. What if a bullet bit through the heavy door?

But he needed to see who was in the hallway. What if the gunman had brought friends?

Kerry rushed into her bedroom and got down on her knees, reaching under the bed for the portable safe she'd purchased to hold her gun. She pulled it out and used the handprint lock to unlock it.

The gun stared up at her, all cold and black and threatening. She couldn't hesitate now, not when their lives were in danger.

She sprinted out of the room and handed the weapon over to Bryan, who'd done some swift rearranging of her furniture. The couch was now in front of the doorway, not blocking the entrance, but a few feet back, giving the door enough room to swing open.

"It's not a barricade," he said, possibly reading her mind. "But I'm going to need cover." He checked the gun, though she didn't know what for. It looked like he knew how to use it. "Our only way out of this is through that door. I'll engage the assailant, and once he's down or out of ammunition, we run. Keep back and out of range of the door. Got it?"

Kerry's heart threatened to beat out of her chest and she gripped Bryan's arm tight. Some instinct was telling her she *had* to touch him. And wasn't that the weirdest thing? She wanted to throw her arms around him and keep him close. The thought of him stepping into the line of fire made sweat break out and the darkness inside of her growl.

But her inner darkness wasn't bullet proof. She was useless against a gun.

"I'm tougher than I look," Bryan assured her. "I'll be fine. Now get into position. And I'm sorry about your door. And your couch."

She didn't have time to ask what he meant, but she could imagine the upholstery wouldn't look good once it was littered with bullet holes.

She braced herself, ready for the shots to start again. Was the gunman right outside the door? How did Bryan think he was going to open it without getting shot? Her mind raced, and she had no answers. Screw the police; if her phone was working she'd call her dad. He knew his way out of a gunfight.

But no one was coming. She and Bryan had to rely on themselves.

Between one blink and the next, her door swung open. Kerry hadn't seen Bryan move, and he was taking cover behind his makeshift fort. Then the shooting started and her ears rang. She smelled fire and the hint of blood, and it made bile rise in her throat.

Even worse when a tall white man, bald and broad and bruiser-like, stepped into the apartment. He darted out just as quickly when Bryan shot. But the angles had to be off. No one was hitting anything.

"When I give the word!" Bryan was yelling, and

Kerry barely heard him. It wasn't even loud, not except for the gunshots.

Kerry nodded frantically and tried not to imagine whether or not they could survive a jump from her apartment windows. Maybe if the awning from the restaurant below was open. Maybe.

But they couldn't run on broken legs.

It wouldn't be a problem for her, but she wouldn't leave Bryan behind.

The gunman shot wildly and fire burned its way through Kerry's shoulder. She cried out, unable to stop the complaint. And Bryan let out an animalistic cry she couldn't comprehend and launched himself over the couch in an impossible burst of speed.

Two more shots. The gunman cried out and there was a crash to the floor.

Bryan rushed back into the apartment. "Can you run?" he asked, breath heavy.

Kerry clutched her hand to her shoulder and grimaced. It felt like something was moving under her skin, worming its way toward the surface, heedless of anything in its path.

Her shoulder was hurt. Not her legs. "I'm good." She grimaced as she said it, but they had to move.

They ran past the gunman who writhed on the floor, blood pooling to one side. Bryan kicked his gun away and they took the stairs in a sprint. Kerry barely avoided slamming into the wall when they took a corner too quickly, but she didn't stop and she didn't complain.

The gunman wasn't dead. And she was almost certain he would come after them.

# CHAPTER NINE

ADRENALINE from the fight had nothing on his need to care for Kerry. The street outside her apartment was a whole world away from the chaos they'd just run through, and no one seemed to realize what had happened.

The smart move would be to stop and call the cops, report shots fired, and hope they arrived sometime before the end of the world. Harper would send people if he knew. This was more confirmation than they could have dreamed of that Kerry was in danger.

Bryan wished Harper had been wrong.

They ran two blocks before Bryan forced them to stop and pushed Kerry into a small alcove beside a trash can. "Let me see it," he said, laying his hand gently over her fingers which clutched her shoulder. It was bloody, but not as bloody as it should have been.

He'd been shot in the shoulder like that and it had nearly killed him. Of course, that had been the silver.

But humans couldn't handle what he could. It was a miracle Kerry could move at all.

"It's not as bad as it looks," she insisted, slowly sliding her fingers down.

"You need a hospital." The words were instinctive, but he didn't think a hospital would be safe. There was no telling who'd sent the gunman or what kind of friends he had.

"I really don't. See?" She shoved her shoulder at him, and he had to rear back before it hit him in the face. "All good."

Her shirt was torn and bloody with the telltale rip where a bullet had gone through. But she wasn't bleeding much and she wasn't holding herself like a person with a bullet in the shoulder. "Something hit you," he said, mind scrambling. Maybe wood from the door or a ricochet.

"It'll be fine." She said it with the confidence of a woman who knew her body.

He'd heard the same confidence from people with gut wounds. It meant nothing. They had to get her to a doctor. Stasia. If he could get to the office in Brooklyn, Stasia could take care of her.

But they had to make sure they didn't lead the gunman straight there. Sure, the man had been bleeding out, but Bryan had a feeling he wouldn't be down for long. There was something about the way the man moved, the way he *smelled*, that made Bryan wonder if he was completely human.

"Let's go." Bryan had a plan now, and they had a destination. That was the best they could do.

They'd only taken a few steps down the street when a hand clamped on his shoulder and a meaty fist slugged him.

Stupid. *Stupid.* Bryan wasn't aware enough of his surroundings and he was going to get himself and Kerry killed.

A growl came from behind him and he didn't understand it, not at first. He chanced a glance at Kerry and saw her eyes had gone yellow and her teeth were too long, the first symptoms of a shift.

"Let. Him. Go." The words were muffled around her teeth. She darted forward and scratched her claws against his assailant, not the gunman, but another man who moved just like him.

The man went down. He and Kerry ran.

Bryan's mind reeled as they sprinted. He looked at

her, but the wolfish features had already bled away, leaving just the human behind.

"Don't freak out on me," she panted as they turned a corner. Kerry raised her hand and a taxi stopped two seconds later. She really *did* have super-powers. She gave an address that he didn't recognize, but it was out of Manhattan, far enough away to give them a moment to regroup. No way their attackers could track a random cab.

The cab driver took a look at them, but something must have held his tongue. He didn't ask why they were panting or why Kerry's shirt was bloody. Then again, in his job, he probably saw a lot of crazy things.

"Let me see your shoulder," he said once they'd settled into traffic and he was at least a little confident that they hadn't been found.

"I told you it's fine." She shifted away from him.

He could still smell the blood. The cab had a small assortment of bottled waters, wet wipes, and hand sanitizer, and he grabbed the wipes. "Even if it's healed, you've still got blood all over you. Let me." He held up the wipes. He could have just handed them over, but something deep inside of him needed to tend to her, to make sure all remained well.

"It was never as bad as it looked. That's all." She said it like she was trying to convince him she hadn't sprouted claws and fought off their attacker. Of course, she had no way of knowing what *he* was.

"I got shot in the shoulder once," he said as he pulled out a wipe and slowly moved his hand towards her shoulder. She unbuttoned the top two buttons of her top and opened it enough to reveal her healing skin. It was an angry red now, the wound mostly closed, but still covered in blood. There was something thick sticking out of her skin. Bryan snagged it with two fingers and pulled it out. She hissed in pain and the wound started bleeding for a moment before closing.

No human could do that.

He held up the bullet for her to see. "The one in me looked similar. But it had a bit of silver lodged in it somehow. Best guess is it impacted a silver candlestick right before it hit me. No one's quite sure. That almost killed me. Until we got the silver out. Then I healed up just like you."

Her eyes widened as he cleaned up the wound. He pressed too hard at first and she winced, her skin still tender.

"What are you telling me?" She covered his hand with hers and took the wipe, folding it neatly and slipping the wet, bloody bundle into her jeans. Good idea. He didn't want anyone getting more of her blood.

"I've got teeth and claws of my own." She wasn't the first shifter outside of his pack that he'd heard of, but she was different. "Do you have a pack?"

Her eyes widened. "For real?"

He nodded. It was strange to be the shifter who actually knew something about their world for once. But three years into this business and he was starting to feel like he had a handle on it.

No doubt that would change. But right now, he reveled. Just a tiny bit.

"For real. I'm guessing you weren't born to it." He shuddered to think what a mob boss who was also a werewolf would be like, but he doubted her dad turned furry. He didn't know much about Roger Delgado, but he had to assume the man was human. It still felt too weird to think of people as human or not human. Bryan didn't think he'd ever get used to it.

"Bitten," she confirmed. They both kept their voices low and the cab driver's music was loud. Even then, he probably wouldn't believe they were actually shifters, even if he did overhear them. "About a year ago. During the shooting."

"You didn't tell anyone." It wasn't a question. He and the others had all been vague about their own strange transformations into wolves. It was a protective instinct to hide something that should be impossible.

"By the time the cops got there, the wound had already healed. At first I thought I had imagined how bad it would be. A few days later, I learned otherwise. When I..." She looked up at the cab driver and clamped her mouth shut, a reminder they weren't alone.

Bryan grabbed her hand and squeezed tight. He wanted to pull her into his arms and promise that everything would be okay, they just had to figure things out. Unfortunately, he had no idea how they were going to do that. So he satisfied himself with her hand and hoped it would be enough.

His heart ached and he knew it wasn't. They'd just met, but he knew he wanted all of her. Needed her.

There was a word for it that threatened to overwhelm him, but he pushed that instinct away. They were on the run from at least two assailants. He couldn't start piling his feelings on her and hope she'd return them.

He needed to take her to Gibson. Gibson could help. She needed to learn what it meant to be a shifter so she didn't get in trouble. Or get hurt.

He remembered the files he'd read that Rowe and Vi had uncovered, the murdered shifters and witches.

Kerry could be a target in more ways than one. And given that she'd been bitten, there could be a werewolf on the loose somewhere in the city.

This whole job had gotten a lot more complicated.

"We need a place to lie low," he said, mostly to say *something*. The cab had a strange way of lulling him into a false sense of security. The outside world couldn't get to them as long as they were in this vehicle.

It was a lie, of course. But it didn't change the fact that it felt true.

"I actually have an idea about that." She caught the cab driver's attention. "Can you pull over up ahead, please? Change of plans."

The man nodded.

She smiled at Bryan. "Let's head to the beach."

# CHAPTER TEN

CRIME PAID and Kerry hated it. She looked up at her father's gorgeous house in Montauk and couldn't help but wonder just how much blood had gone into the foundation. Not literally.

Probably.

He wouldn't bury his enemies so close to home. Not even his vacation home.

The one bright side of her father's call that afternoon was that she was sure he wasn't *here*. He'd been off doing business at his place in New Jersey and had no reason to come to the Hamptons.

She had a key, the security codes, and a standing invitation to use the house whenever he wasn't there. She'd never taken him up on it before, but desperate times called for desperate measures.

The two hour long train ride out had been mostly silent. With so many commuters around them, they couldn't talk about anything real. Bryan had snagged her a new t-shirt at a tourist shop and it wasn't stylish, but it did invite fewer questions than the shirt covered in blood.

The sun had only just set and that was screwing with her head more than anything. Five hours ago, she never would have thought she'd be running for her life with a werewolf bodyguard at her side.

And yet, here she was.

He was a freaking *werewolf*. Just like her.

She had so many questions she wanted to ask, explanations and everything else. But the words caught on her tongue. She'd spent the two hour train ride staring silently at the book she'd purchased at a newsstand and hoping something would start making sense.

But no. Everything was just as messed up as it was before they climbed on the train.

"There should be something for us to eat in the pantry. Dad usually keeps at least a few cans of soup or some rice on hand, just in case he ends up here unexpectedly. And there should be some clothes for both of us. We can head to the store in the morning. Figure things out from there." The tourist shirt was surprisingly soft, but Kerry still wanted to peel it off and stand under a shower head for an hour or three. Blood had crusted on her skin and it itched.

"Do you know how to set up the security system?" Bryan asked, eyes scanning the road behind them as if the gunman they'd faced would suddenly teleport in and finish the job.

Then again, maybe Kerry shouldn't be so blasé about that. She was a werewolf. Who was to say that teleporters didn't exist?

"Yeah, we can lock this place down tight. Once it's on, if anyone tries to come in, we'll hear the alarm and it will send a signal to my dad's people. They'll come running." She led him up the path to the door and unlocked it before finding the security panel and punching in her code. She tried to hide how thankful she was that it actually worked. Now would be a terrible time to find out her dad had lied about using the house.

"Your dad's people?" Bryan prompted.

Kerry pursed her lips, a lifetime's worth of silence that couldn't be broken with one soft question. She'd learned since she was a toddler that she wasn't supposed to say anything specific about her dad's work. He was a *businessman*. He did *business*. That was all anyone needed to know.

But Bryan was supposed to be a bodyguard and he needed to know just a little more. And given that he'd spoken to Detective Harper, he might already. Her father had never gone to jail, but some of his people had. There were always rumors.

She wouldn't spread gossip.

"He has security people. He trusts them to prioritize his needs more than he trusts the cops. Hopefully no one comes looking for us and they don't get called." Her hand hovered over the control panel. "I can leave the system off, but then we won't get the alarms."

"Turn it on. We can use any help we can get."

Kerry did. Then she led him on the shortest tour of the house she could manage. Kitchen. Bedrooms. Entertainment room. Office. "There's a pool outside," she added, "but we need to stay inside if we don't want to set the alarm off ourselves. And it's a bit chilly for swimming."

Bryan looked out the window into the swiftly darkening night. He had an intense look on his face and Kerry wondered what he saw that she didn't. She didn't ask. "If you're good to go, I'm going upstairs to take a shower. You can sleep in any room except for the master bedroom or whichever one I'm in. Sounds good?"

"Do you think your dad has any phone chargers laying around?" He held up his phone. "I'm running low on charge."

"There should be some in one of the kitchen drawers. Grab one for me if there are two. It looks like we have similar phones." Her own phone had to be on its last legs, but Kerry cared more about a shower at the moment.

Bryan didn't delay her any longer.

The climb up the stairs was like summiting Everest. She may have had werewolf superpowers, but that didn't mean she didn't *also* experience the body aches that came from a combination of using those superpowers and exhaustion.

The bed in the room she chose called to her with an all too tempting siren song, and Kerry was tempted to throw herself down on the fluffy mattress and surrender to oblivion. But she wanted her shower just that much more.

She stripped off her clothes and was glad to see there was soap, shampoo, and conditioner already in the shower waiting for her to use them. She let the water run hot and stepped under the spray, wincing as it bit into her tender skin.

But she didn't change the temperature. She

wanted that top layer of her skin flayed off, the memory of the day taken with it.

Kerry ran her fingers over her shoulder, searching for the spot the bullet had hit her. But her skin was as smooth as ever, not even tender where she thought she'd been hit. An inhuman sound caught in her throat, suffering and fear and the relief of survival all rolled into one.

She shouldn't have survived the day. Without Bryan by her side, she wouldn't have. And her mind was just catching up to that fact. She was so beyond lucky that she might actually be blessed.

It took her a moment to realize the wetness on her face was tears and not the spray of the shower.

Kerry hiccupped out one sob after another as her emotions assailed her. She was supposed to be happy to be alive, but all she could think of now was what would have happened if that bullet had hit closer to her heart. Would she survive it?

What if the attacker had a machine gun or something worse? What if he found them?

By the time she was clean, the tears hadn't stopped. Kerry turned the water off with a jerk of her hand and crumpled down to the ground, clutching her legs tight and letting the sobs take her.

## CHAPTER ELEVEN

Bryan stayed up late that night, but he had to surrender to sleep sometime. An exhausted guard would be no use to his charge. He couldn't get a hold of Gibson, so he left a brief message on his voicemail. He didn't give away their location, just in case Gibson's phone got compromised somehow, but he let his alpha know that the job was proceeding in an unexpected way.

And long after midnight he slept.

He tried not to think of the sobs he'd heard coming from Kerry's bathroom when he ducked inside her chosen room to put a phone charger on her nightstand. His wolf almost took over and dragged him across the room, and it took all of his self-control to stay in place.

She wouldn't want him to see her like that. Not when she was so vulnerable. Not when they were practically strangers.

*You're not strangers. She's your…*

He cut the thought off. He'd almost slept on the floor outside her room, as if he was worried about attackers from within. Instead, he'd taken the bedroom across the hall. And when he woke up early the next morning, Kerry was silent. He poked his head inside her room to make sure she was still there and found her sleeping.

For the first time since they'd met, she looked peaceful. Her pale skin practically glowed in the dim room as if she was lit by her own inner fire. An inner fire that was reflected in the red of her hair.

Bryan forced himself to take a step back and close the door. If he looked at her for any longer it would get creepy. His inner wolf didn't understand that and he didn't have time to explain. Not that he actually *could* explain something to that part of him. It wasn't really some separate entity, not the way he sometimes thought of it. He was his wolf and his wolf was him.

But it hurt his head to think about it sometimes.

So Bryan didn't.

Needing to do something productive, he headed to the kitchen. He'd crashed the night before without eating anything, and his stomach was demanding immediate repayment for that misstep. And just as Kerry had suspected, there was a pantry filled with shelf stable foods. He peeked in the refrigerator and saw a six pack of beer and a filtered pitcher full of water.

Could be worse.

He pulled out a box of oatmeal packets and what appeared to be powdered eggs. The eggs sounded gross, but maybe he wasn't being optimistic enough.

A minute in the microwave later, his nose informed him he'd been *way* too optimistic. No way was he eating the eggs.

The oatmeal was okay, though.

Kerry came down a bit later wearing gray sweatpants and a plain black t-shirt that hung off her frame like she was a child. The shirt was meant for someone bouncer sized. Even Bryan would be engulfed by it.

"There's oatmeal," he said, and slid the box her way. "Stay away from the eggs."

She shuddered. "Yeah, I could smell them from my room. No thanks." But she prepared her own bowl of oatmeal and they ate in silence.

Bryan dove back into the pantry while Kerry ate, in search of coffee before realizing he hadn't seen a coffee maker on the counter. But in a rich person house like this, it was probably hidden behind a wall panel or something. Wouldn't want people to actually think the kitchen was ever used for cooking.

"Coffee maker?" he asked when he stepped back out of the walk in pantry.

Kerry grimaced and shook her head. "Dad doesn't drink coffee. Won't have it in any of his houses. You might find some herbal tea in one of the cupboards."

"No coffee?" He didn't mean to whine, and he could feel his cheeks heat at the sound of his voice.

Kerry shook her head again and finished her breakfast.

Bryan had to bite back a quip about her dad. He wasn't going to make jokes about a mob boss to his daughter in his house. He wasn't that stupid.

He checked the clock and looked out the window. It was only a little after six and still dark out, though the sky would rapidly lighten. But it was the off season and this part of town was practically deserted. "Let's go for a run." He bounced on his feet as he said it, his wolf perking up.

Kerry stared at him. "I'm not exactly a jogger. And I don't have sneakers."

A grin pulled at his lips. "No sneakers."

Her stare was blank for a moment before realization dawned. "We can't. Someone will see."

"We'll keep to those woods in the yard, more or less. And no one will question a couple of dogs on the road. We need it after yesterday." It hadn't even been forty-eight hours since Bryan's last wolfish run, but desire beat at him hard. He wanted to see Kerry in her other form. Would her pelt be the same as her hair, like some fox transformed into a wolf? Would she be as graceful on four legs as she was on two?

Suddenly he wanted this run more than he wanted his next breath, and he'd make a deal with any devil to make sure it happened.

But it only took her a second to agree. "If we end up in the pound, I'm definitely blaming you. Let me set the security system so we can leave. Meet me out behind the pool house. I'll be there in five minutes."

Bryan practically skipped out there, waiting only long enough for Kerry to turn off the security system before heading out. It took no time to find the pool house. He skirted around the pool and shucked off his clothes after looking around to make sure he wasn't being watched.

Though he wouldn't mind if Kerry saw him naked.

But she was still inside, and given her suggestion, Bryan realized she probably wanted to shift in private. That was fine. He'd see her other form soon enough.

The change came over him quickly, one exquisite

moment of pain as his senses exploded out of him and he reformed into the beast that was his other self. He knew he was big for a wolf, all his pack was. As far as he knew, it was true for all shifters. His fur would be gray and his eyes yellow. And his teeth were more than big enough to scare any Little Red Riding Hoods that wandered down his path.

He smelled Kerry before he saw her, and he wanted to roll around in her scent until he was coated with it. She smelled of the wild earth and wandering and home, things he couldn't quantify but knew he needed.

And when she walked around the corner he stood in awe. Her fur wasn't the same red of her hair. Instead it was golden, with red and brown strands working their way through it. She was her own wolfish ray of sunshine and he wanted to bask in it. And though it should have been impossible, it was her eyes that remained the same, emeralds in a wolfish face.

She came to a stop just out of pouncing range and studied him for several seconds. Bryan stood as tall as he could on four legs and hoped he met her expectations. He knew he was a fine specimen of a wolf and he wanted her to appreciate it.

But the sun was rising fast and they wouldn't have

much time for their run if they wasted it admiring each other.

They could do that later.

He barked at her once before taking off across the yard. And then came the first shock of the day. Kerry streaked past him as if she'd been running on four legs all her life and lived for the chase.

It was on.

Bryan sped up, no longer playing nice. He nipped at her heels as they dove into the woods and overtook her between one breath and the next. But she didn't let him keep the lead for long.

Bryan was fast and an experienced wolf, more experienced than her, anyway, but Kerry knew these woods better than him, and he was almost shocked out of his skin when she appeared in front of him and plowed into his side, nipping playfully and prancing over him in a burst of speed.

As they got closer to the road and civilization, their playful race turned into a companionable walk. They didn't need the local humans seeing two huge wolves fighting on the side of the highway.

But Bryan wondered what it would be like to run with Kerry on Gibson's farm, where they had hundreds of acres to roam as they pleased. Their play wouldn't have to stop after only a few minutes out in the country.

He couldn't tell time with any accuracy while in his fur, but the sun had climbed overhead by the time they headed back to the house. They hunkered down behind the pool house, but Bryan was in no hurry to shift back.

Running as a wolf was fun, but laying down and enjoying the ground underneath him and the weight of this different body was just as enjoyable. Especially when Kerry lay down right beside him.

He could live in this moment for the rest of forever and call himself happy.

They lay like that for a long time and Bryan felt no urgency at shifting back or returning to their human troubles. Worries had a way of feeling distant in this form. He didn't have to think about outside threats or what the feelings churning inside him for Kerry meant. He could just lay quietly and enjoy the way her scent mingled with his as they basked in the sun.

But they couldn't lay down forever.

Just a little more time wouldn't hurt.

He drifted off to sleep, promising some invisible force that it would only be for a few minutes. It was too hard to resist the temptation of a nap while he wore his fur. But no nap could last forever.

When he woke, it was to find he'd slipped out of his fur and back into his human skin. It happened sometimes, though he'd never yet fallen asleep as a man and woken up a wolf.

Kerry was next to him, pale skin on display, and he forced himself to look no further than her shoulders. And hoped *she* wouldn't look south either. Or, if she did, that she'd like what she'd see.

His body was on fire for her, hot and hard and ready for more. But he forced himself to stay still. If he were a stronger man, he would have gotten up and walked away right then. He wasn't here to kiss her. He had a job to do.

But her lips were so red in the sunlight he could almost taste them.

She blinked her eyes open and their gazes locked. Her eyes darted down and stopped on his lips. Her tongue darted out to wet her own.

And Bryan only had so much willpower.

They met in the middle, mouths coming together in a meeting that felt guided by the hand of fate. Bryan's fingers threaded through her hair and cradled her head, holding her close as his tongue swept into her mouth and tangled with hers.

He lost himself in the kiss. He could stay here all day and damn the consequences.

The loud *bang* of a gunshot pulled him out of the kiss and he jumped to his feet, spinning around and looking for the threat. But a moment later he heard a groaning engine and realized it was a car backfiring.

No one was shooting at them.

Not yet. Not again.

But Bryan had been so distracted, anyone could have snuck up on them and they'd be goners.

He looked towards the house and then back down at Kerry, who was shuffling to her feet and angling her body so he didn't see her front. He forced himself to look away.

"We should head inside." His voice came out more gruff than he meant, but he started walking before she could respond.

He couldn't let his attraction to her get them killed.

# CHAPTER TWELVE

BRYAN DISAPPEARED into the house when they got back and Kerry didn't try to stop him. She could still feel the imprint of his lips on hers and was tempted to follow him up to his bedroom and see just how far they could take things between them.

He made her burn. She wanted the flame.

But she didn't want him running hot and cold on her. And if *that* little display out back was any hint of what might be coming their way, she didn't need any part of it. She didn't play games.

*He's keeping you safe.*

That pesky thought made her scowl. She'd kept herself safe for twenty-five years. More or less. Or, if not for her entire life, then certainly since she'd been on her own after she left college. Yeah, her dad had a hand in funding the gallery, but it wasn't like he had security breathing down her neck. She looked out for herself.

But no one had hunted her down to shoot her before. The shooting she'd witnessed hadn't been about her, she'd just been a bystander and a witness. Yesterday was different.

And if it weren't for Bryan, she would have been shot. Or worse.

What if that man hadn't been coming to kill her? There were other options. Kidnapping. Rape. Torture.

She had to sit down on the kitchen stool as her legs threatened to give out. She adjusted the robe she'd slipped into once she got inside and looked at the clock. It was later than she thought. Though they'd only run until a little after sunrise, it was now close to ten AM. They must have slept for a while.

It probably wasn't the wisest move, but she couldn't regret it. Not when she felt more relaxed than she had in a year. She turned her mind away from the threat and back to the run and to the good part of yesterday. She hadn't realized she might ever meet another werewolf.

Most days she liked to pretend that *she* wasn't a werewolf. She'd only seen the wolf that attacked her at the moment of the attack. She didn't have any sort of wolfy-sense that drew her to others who were like her. So Bryan might be her only shot at learning about what she was.

She didn't fool herself into thinking that the wolfiness could be undone. After a year of this, that felt completely impossible. And she was more or less okay with that. She didn't think she was a monster or bound for hell just because she grew fur every so often and howled at the moon.

But she hadn't realized how much the secret had been weighing on her. She hadn't gone on a date in a year, too afraid that she might give her weirdness away. Combined with the nightmares the attack and the shooting had given her, she'd drawn into herself until she may as well have locked herself up and thrown away the key.

She had friends. Or she used to. They'd been in touch after they found out about the shooting, but Kerry had cut them off. She couldn't explain it. And she wasn't supposed to talk about what she'd seen. And telling her dad was right out. Best case scenario, he'd throw her in a mental institution, worst case scenario, he'd believe her and use her.

She wished her mom was still alive. She would have understood. Or at least tried.

Kerry swiped at her eyes before tears could try to

form. She was supposed to be thinking about how fun it was to run with her bodyguard, not dwell on how pathetic her life had become.

She took two deep breaths and let them out, releasing the negative energy in a way a long ago therapist had taught her. She didn't have to let her emotions control her.

It was a good thought. A great thought, even. Until her phone rang and the name on the caller ID shattered that.

Her hand hovered over the device for a moment and she was tempted to chuck it across the room. But she was sitting in her father's house and wearing clothes she'd borrowed from him. She couldn't just ignore this.

"What are you doing in the Hamptons?" her father demanded before she'd finished her greeting.

Kerry ground her teeth together and didn't bother trying to release the negative energy. *That* might lead to a nuclear explosion. She'd try and diffuse it later. "You told me I could use the house." She tried to keep her tone even. Getting snippy with her father would only make things worse.

"I expected you to clear it with me first." She heard muffled sounds in the background and his voice was far away for a moment, as if he'd pressed his phone to his chest to block the mic. Then he came back. "I need you out of that house as soon as possible. And you'd better clean it up before you go. I promised a friend he could use the place and I expect it to be empty and spotless before he gets there."

*I'm your daughter.* The words got caught in her throat and she didn't dare say them. She didn't want to hear his response. Business came first for Roger Delgado. It had to.

And before she could make a reply, the call cut off. Kerry stared at the receiver and wondered if her father had actually hung up on her or if it was an accident.

She wasn't about to call back and see. She didn't want to know.

They'd have to leave. Fine. But before Kerry could shift herself off the stool and go to find Bryan, her phone rang again.

Michaels.

This had to be good.

"Where the hell are you?" Ms. Michaels asked, and it was disconcerting just how closely her tone matched Kerry's father.

"Hello," Kerry responded. Since she didn't know where she was going to be in an hour, she wasn't sure the ADA needed to know her exact location. And she had no idea who was gunning for her. Could she trust the ADA?

"Harper just sent me a report of shots fired at your apartment last night and you're nowhere to be seen. There's security footage of you running away with that alleged bodyguard and being chased by a bald giant. You need to get your ass to my office and explain everything to me and Harper before this gets even more out of control. I want you here in an hour." Unlike her father, Michaels gave Kerry a chance to respond.

"I'm not in the city," Kerry said. "I can't be there in an hour. And I'm not sure it's safe. Bryan said he saw the man that attacked us in your office building."

"Are you suggesting that I sent a gunman to your apartment?" Michaels had the kind of voice that would make the guilty shit their pants. No wonder she was so good at her job.

"No. You could take care of me way more easily than that. And you have no reason to. But the city doesn't feel safe at the moment and I'm not sure I should go back. I don't want whoever sent those gunmen to find me." She flinched as she remembered the bang of the guns firing and the burnt smell in the air.

"You're talking to me on your cell phone. The only

reason I haven't tracked you down yet is that I need a warrant. Someone who isn't bound by the law will find you even sooner. They may be on their way to you now. Come back and I can protect you. This kind of threat means we can get an actual police protective unit authorized. No need for some two-bit body-guard." There was a brief pause. "Did you say *gunmen*? As in more than one?"

They didn't know? They weren't competent enough to identify more than one attacker and they thought they could keep her safe?

Yeah, right.

"I'll get in touch when we're heading back to the city." She just didn't know *when* that would be.

"Don't make me come find you. Your case is about to run off a cliff and I don't want you to get hurt in the fallout." Michaels ended the call.

Kerry stared at her phone for several moments. There it was. This wasn't about her safety. It was about her damned testimony. That was all Michaels cared about. She had such tunnel vision that she didn't seem to realize that Kerry feared for her *life*.

She shut off her cell phone and was tempted to find a hammer to smash it with. Michaels was right about that, at least. And she was surprised Bryan hadn't thought about it.

Her stomach growled, a reminder that a bit of oatmeal wasn't really enough for a werewolf's always hungry stomach. They had to get moving, and they could find food later.

She only hoped that Bryan had some idea of where they could go.

# CHAPTER THIRTEEN

The more Kerry thought about it, the worse things got. And by the time she was done showering off her run and changing into clothes that would have to do, her hands shook. Her stomach roiled, thoughts of hunger pushed away by panic.

They had to move. Someone could already be coming for her. What if whoever had sent those gunmen had already tracked her phone? She should have chucked it into the Hudson before they had the chance.

Bryan had been taking a shower of his own when she came upstairs, but the water was off now and the house strangely silent. Her father's friends would be here sometime and she didn't want to meet them. The people he called friends were all as slimy as they came and even worse than he was. She didn't want to make small talk or answer questions.

What would happen if gunman attacked the house and only her father's people were here?

She was tempted to call him and warn him, but a dark part of her said that he'd gotten her into this mess in the first place. If she hadn't been moving mysterious boxes for his associates, no one would have attacked the gallery.

She'd stopped trafficking in those crates and her father hadn't insisted that she start up again. But that wouldn't last forever.

His men could handle themselves. And hopefully no gunmen would come.

She heard Bryan's footsteps before he stopped in front of her slightly open door and knocked on the frame, pushing it further open so he could lean in the doorway. "Hey," he said softly.

Her mind flashed back to the kiss, her body suddenly hot before a cold wave of dread washed over her. They'd been out in the open back there. Someone with a sniper rifle could have taken them out. And neither of them would have seen it coming.

What were they *thinking?*

Stupid werewolf hormones were going to get them killed.

"We need to clear out." She tried to sound calm, commanding. In control. Her voice didn't shake, so she was calling it a win. "My father called. He's loaned this house to a friend and expects us gone before his guests get here."

"How did he know we were here?" Bryan didn't move into the room, and his voice was all business. Maybe he was trying to pretend the kiss hadn't happened.

Good. They could both pretend and go back to a purely business relationship. One hurdle down.

*Liar*, the voice that sounded a lot like her inner wolf whispered. *He's ours.*

She wanted him to be. So bad it hurt. But Kerry knew how to deny herself, knew how to deal with not getting what she wanted. This was no different.

"I assume there was an alert to his security team when I used my code to get in. The code is specific to me, and there are cameras by the entrances. He would have access to that footage." It hadn't seemed like a big deal last night.

"Cameras?" Bryan straightened. "Did he see us run? Does he *know?*"

There was a thread of panic in his voice and it strangely helped her calm down a little. Only one of them could afford to freak out at a time. "I disabled the cameras before we ran. And guests disable the cameras out here all the time for a variety of reasons. It shouldn't cause any alarm."

"I hope you're right."

"Me too." Of course, disabling the cameras around the pool house might make her father wonder what she'd gotten up to in the pool, especially when her guest was as sexy as Bryan Vega. Let him wonder. He'd never guess the truth. "And he doesn't know. About me. Would it be a problem if he did? Are there werewolf police or something?" She'd tried searching information out online, but after finding mostly romance novels or fetish content, she'd had to back off.

Werewolvesarereal.com had, unsurprisingly, been an unreliable resource.

"I haven't met any werewolf police," Bryan admitted. "Though, apparently the correct word is shifter. Just found that out. I'll tell you the story later. Sounds like we need to clear out."

"Yeah." She didn't want to move, though. She wanted to ask Bryan more questions about what it meant to be a shifter. Had he been born to it? It didn't sound that way. But they had to get out of the house before her father's friend arrived. "Michaels wants me at her office. The police came to my apartment last night."

"Fuck!" It was a bit of an overreaction to her comment, but she understood when he kept talking. "You still have your phone. It could have been traced. Shit. You need to turn it off. Now. And we need to dump it. But best to do it once we've left. We don't want to accidentally lead anyone to your father's people. Right?"

"The phone is off." She pointed to a small box sitting on her bedside table. "I got that thing for Dad as a joke a few years ago. Apparently it blocks all phone signals. I figure it's an extra layer of protection in case the phone can still be tracked while it's turned off." Her voice was still steady, but she could feel the edge of panic creeping up again. "Do you think someone's tracking us?"

He considered it for a moment before shaking his head. "Not really. We've been here for more than twelve hours. Plenty of time to take us out. They hit you at your apartment, that's not a difficult address to find. But I say that once we're in transit, we find a place to put your phone, turn it on, and leave it there. If someone's tracking us, it might buy us a bit of time."

She hoped that was true. She needed *something* to go her way. The echo of the shots kept ricocheting around her mind and she couldn't help but imagine what would have happened if she'd been hit.

Or Bryan.

*No!*

It wasn't her inner voice that said that, but the wolf's. Or maybe they were both her. It was all jumbled inside of her and she couldn't make sense of it. At some point she'd stopped trying. But the thought of Bryan shot and bleeding out, of dying for her... no, she couldn't have that.

"I'll meet you downstairs in fifteen minutes," she said. She had to cut this conversation off before she started actively freaking out. And what if he brought up their run? Their kiss? Yeah, this conversation had to end.

Now.

He hesitated for a moment before nodding and leaving her alone.

Kerry's window looked out onto the backyard of the property. She couldn't see if anyone was coming, but she could feel the clock ticking down. It wouldn't be the end of the world if her father's associate spotted her. It was no secret she was Roger Delgado's daughter. But she didn't want to be drawn into anything else.

She'd witnessed enough crimes for one lifetime.

There wasn't much to pack, and tidying the room didn't take long. The room was as spotless as she could make it, and she still had a few minutes to spare. Kerry was tempted to hang around and take those precious minutes for herself, to try and find her center and make sense of the world around her.

But the sooner they left, the sooner this would be over.

She hoped.

She slipped the box with her phone in it into her purse and headed downstairs. Her bloody shirt was in a plastic bag she'd fished out from under the kitchen sink and she wanted to burn it, rather than carry it with her. Magic was real, even realer than she'd dared imagine, and she wasn't sure she should be leaving bloody clothes around for anyone to find.

At the very least it was unhygienic. But what if some wizard could use her blood to control her or something?

*That* question was going to the top of the list. She needed to know if she should be incinerating her tampons. Or maybe she'd have to start using a menstrual cup. Despite herself, she grinned. Bryan was definitely going to enjoy this conversation.

Bryan waited for her in the front hall, a serious look on his face.

"Problem?" she asked, stomach sinking. Maybe she hadn't turned her phone off in time, after all.

"Company."

She looked out the door and saw two black sedans pull into the driveway and cut off any avenue of escape.

# CHAPTER FOURTEEN

Kerry let out a stream of curses that had Bryan mildly impressed. He hadn't heard anything that fluent since he'd left the service. Kerry's gun was hidden in the small bag he carried. With no holster and strict laws about taking weapons on public transportation, hiding it had been the best option.

Now his fingers itched for the cool metal.

"I know that guy." Kerry was looking out the window, and Bryan had to stop himself from yanking her back.

He really sucked at this bodyguard thing and he was going to get her killed if he didn't step up. "Know him how?" he asked, stepping closer and shouldering her aside so she was no longer in the line of fire. "Are these your dad's friends?"

He saw a dark-haired man in his forties who looked vaguely familiar, but he was turned so Bryan only saw his profile. The people around him were all strangers, though.

"I think so. He's some super rich guy. Runs a corporation or something." She scrunched her face up and then snapped her fingers. "Selby."

"AR Selby?" He wanted the gun even more now, with apologies to Stasia for wanting to shoot her brother. But there was a growing possibility the man was involved with whatever had gotten him turned into a shifter and led to the disappearances of a bunch of people on the East Coast.

"We've met a few times. He and my dad have a business relationship." She shot him an overly confident grin. "Let me handle this. We just need to walk past them and head for the road. The train station isn't far."

"We need a car." Gibson's farm was the safest place to go for now. It had no connection to Kerry or her family and no one would track them there.

He hoped.

Gibson might kill him if he compromised the place.

"There's a car rental place near the train station," she offered.

It was better than nothing. Bryan studied the people milling around AR Selby for a moment. He spotted holsters under the arms of two men in slim fitting dark suits. AR didn't appear to be armed, but the scion of a billionaire's empire wouldn't do his own dirty work. There were three other people who appeared to be unarmed, but Bryan wouldn't count on that.

And there was no telling if AR had shifters or witches with him. Bryan didn't know for sure if AR knew about the supernatural, but the chances seemed greater by the day that he might. His own sisters were shifters. Did he know that? Or were Stasia and Em still keeping that secret?

"If this goes to shit, stay with me," he warned. "We'll make for the woods behind the house and run through the forest. Even on two legs we should be faster than normal people. Our goal will be to make for the train station and get on whatever train is leaving right then. If we get split up or something happens to me, keep running and get to the nearest police station and try and get in touch with Harper and Michaels."

"Nothing is going to happen to you." The ferocity in her voice was a surprise and made his own wolf growl in agreement. "Let's do this."

She threw the door open and walked out the front of the house. AR and his people all turned their way, and one of the armed men casually reached under his shoulder but didn't pull his weapon.

"Kerry?" AR asked, shielding his eyes from the sun and stepping a bit closer. The other armed man stepped with him, a dangerous shadow.

Kerry pasted a big smile on her face, and between one step and the next somehow transformed into a different person. Her voice went up in pitch and bordered on bubbly. She sounded exactly like the spoiled daughter of crime someone might expect her to be. "Mr. Selby!" The woman actually *giggled* and Bryan had to clamp down on his own expression to keep from giving them away. "You've made Daddy mad at me." Her pout deserved an award.

AR grinned and looked over at Bryan. Then he did a double take before firmly looking back at Kerry. Had Bryan been recognized? AR Selby knew Gibson well enough that he'd called in a favor a year ago to have Gibson send Owen to guard Stasia when she'd nearly been kidnapped. No doubt Selby had done his research about Gibson's guards, but they kept a low profile.

But a man with Selby's resources could find information no one else could.

Bryan plastered his own grin on his face and slung an arm around Kerry. He didn't want AR thinking she was in danger. And there was a simple enough reason why two consenting adults would be holed up in Delgado's Hampton's hideaway. "Me and Kerry here were supposed to be having a fun weekend. You should have seen the bikini she brought."

He deserved a punch in the gut for that remark, but instead she giggled. "You're terrible!"

AR smiled along with them. "I'm sorry for interrupting your fun. Your father told me the house would be empty."

Kerry rolled her eyes. "Like I'm gonna tell *him* why I'm here. It's no big deal. We'll go crash at one of my friend's places." Kerry looked around at AR's people and her gaze snagged on one of them before she pulled her attention back to AR. "We cleaned the place up for you."

"You're a dear." He held up a hand and one of his people stepped forward. "I can have my driver take you to your friend's house. For the imposition."

"Nah." Kerry brushed it off with a shake of her head, leaning into Bryan's side. "It's a pretty walk. And it's so nice out. We don't want to miss it. Come on, babe." She tugged on his arm and started walking. Bryan followed along as if he had nothing better to do than be pulled down the driveway by a spoiled princess.

Really, it wasn't so bad.

AR didn't insist on offering the ride, but Bryan barely breathed until they were two streets away, their feet eating up the distance at a pace just shy of a run. The smile fell off of Kerry's face and her posture slumped. She let go of Bryan's arm and put a bit of space between them.

"There. That went okay." She ran her fingers through her hair and cradled the back of her head. "Though I don't think I'm cut out for espionage. Or acting."

Despite himself, he laughed. "I think you did amazing. I bought it."

Her face grew serious. "I'm not some spoiled princess. But that's who my dad's associates expect me to be. They'll notice me if I'm different. If I'm exactly what they expect, I'm basically a ghost."

Bryan stepped close and lightly placed his hands on her shoulders. "I said I bought it, not that I think that's who you are. I know you better than that." Their gazes locked for a moment and it took a monumental effort not to drop his eyes down to her lips, especially when her own look dropped. The taste of her was imprinted on his memory and he would carry it with him always.

He wanted another. And another. Kisses upon kisses until there was no counting them, until kissing Kerry was just a fact of his existence. He was Bryan Vega and his lips belonged to Kerry Delgado.

*Mate.*

The word had been hovering at the edge of his awareness for some time now and he'd resisted. He was here to do a job, not fall in love. But one look at Kerry and something in him just *knew* that they belonged together. He wasn't sure if the wolf was running the show here or if they would have fallen together even without their furry counterparts, but he wasn't letting her go.

He couldn't.

It would be so easy to lean down and seal their lips together. The street was deserted. They'd made it out of danger. It would only take a second.

But when he kissed Kerry, he wouldn't stop. And he'd already risked enough on one kiss today.

He forced himself to step back, and the space between them felt like the Grand Canyon. "Come on. We need to get out of here."

Kerry nodded and they kept walking. Renting the car was no issue and they were on the road in no time after a quick detour to pick up lunch and a stop at a convenience store for road trip snacks.

Once they were back in the car, Kerry pulled out the bag of licorice that Bryan had insisted on buying and glared at it. "This stuff tastes like cherry flavored plastic. It's gross."

Bryan held out a hand and, despite her objections, she handed him two sticks. He chewed gleefully. "My mom always insists on getting this stuff when we drive for more than a few hours. We drove down to South Carolina once to go to vacation at Myrtle Beach and I swear I ate six pounds of this. I'm basically thirty percent licorice at this point." He took another bite. "And yes, it does taste like cherry flavored plastic. That's part of the appeal."

She pulled a stick out and gave it a sniff before shuddering and stuffing it back in the bag. "No, thank you."

"More for me." He took the bag for himself and stuffed it in between his seat and the center console, a giant grin on his face. The disgusted sound she made shouldn't have made him want to grin even broader or lean over and kiss her, but it took most of his discipline to resist the temptation.

*Later.*

Would there be a later? Could there? It was his job

to keep her safe, not fall for her. And yet, here he was, wanting to sink to his knees and beg her to give him a chance.

The car ate up the miles, and they listened to the radio. They'd been on the road for more than an hour when Kerry finally asked, "So where are we going?"

"Pennsylvania." He hadn't told Gibson they were coming, but that shouldn't be an issue. The farm was the second home for everyone in the pack, and Gibson didn't need to give his permission. But Bryan would call when they got a little closer.

"Any particular part of Pennsylvania? Or are you just going to wing it?" She reached across the console and plucked a strip of licorice from his bag, twirling it around in the air but not eating it.

"My boss has a farm. Lots of acreage. We like to run out there. It's in the middle of nowhere and no one bothers us." He wanted to run with Kerry again, and the farm was as safe a place as he could imagine.

"Run as in *run?*" She stopped twirling the licorice. "So your boss is... like us? Who's we?" The hunger for information sank deep into her words, and Bryan could sate it.

He wanted to sate a lot of things for Kerry. But it was a bit difficult to do most of them while he was driving.

He didn't know if he should be talking about it to Kerry, but he wasn't about to stop himself. She'd been alone for a year, trying to figure out all it meant to be a shifter without any support. At least he'd had the others. They'd been in the dark together. And now he could shed light for someone else.

"I have a pack, I guess you could call it." Even more than three years later it felt a little silly to use words that belonged on a nature documentary. "We were all in the Army together and were abducted off the base we were stationed at in Germany. I'm still not exactly sure what was done to us. We weren't attacked by wolves or anything. I was unconscious for most of it. But there was chanting, and magic. Then we were all dumped back at the base. The military decided to cover it up and discharged us. We stuck together, and a couple months later it was the full moon, we were at Gibson's farm, and we all transformed. Ever since then we've been trying to figure out what exactly we are."

She took a moment to digest that. "How many people are in your pack?"

"Seven of us to start with. Then Owen met Stasia and she... uh, became a wolf on accident. And Andre brought Em in and she's a wolf too. Ten if you count Rowe's mate, but she's a witch, not a wolf." Vi had given the pack so much information about who and what they were that Bryan wouldn't dare omit her. Plus she could get kind of scary and would definitely use her magic against him.

"What does it mean? Became a wolf on accident? Was she captured too? What happened?" Kerry had angled her body completely his way and had started absently chomping on her licorice, so caught up in his story she didn't seem to notice.

Bryan could feel heat rising in his cheeks and wanted to change the subject. "I was injured. Silver in a bullet wound, not a silver bullet; I'm not sure if those exist. She's a doctor and came to help me. Once the silver was extracted, I went a little crazy and bit her. Accidentally. She turned." He tried to keep his voice light, tried not to let on that he'd had nightmares about the incident for months after it happened. He could have killed Stasia and all she'd tried to do was help him.

Kerry must have sensed it was a sensitive topic. She didn't press.

She was quiet for so long that he thought she was done talking. Then she spoke. "Mate?"

That one word had his wolf perking up and trying to wrench control, even in his human form. Bryan gripped the steering wheel tight. "That's another shifter thing. Apparently." Did he sound as cool as he was trying to sound? No way in hell.

"Hmm." She let it drop.

But now there was an awareness to the silence between them, a possibility his wolf knew to be true and he didn't want to deny.

*Mate.*

# CHAPTER FIFTEEN

Kerry's muscles were stiff by the time they made it to the farm, and it felt like they'd been driving for days, rather than a few hours.

"Make yourself comfortable," Bryan told her as he pulled his phone out of his pocket. "I have some calls to make. You can use any of the bedrooms. The only restaurant around here is a pizza place, so we can get some food later. And there should be food in the fridge and pantry. Someone's usually out here at least once a week." He walked outside and Kerry was alone.

She looked around. It was a nice farm house, with plenty of space for the two of them, though she thought it would be a bit crowded for a pack of ten. But the land outside made it worth it. Acres and acres of farm and forest, wild enough for a bunch of wolves to run to their hearts' content.

No wonder there was someone on the property so often. They couldn't resist it.

But for now, her own inner wolf wasn't begging to be let out. The run that morning had sated the beast.

Instead, Kerry could only think of what Bryan had revealed on the drive. A whole pack of shifters. Witches. Evil magic users.

Mates.

That word echoed in her head and resonated with something in her heart. It felt too big to contemplate. And too present.

When Bryan said that word, she could almost imagine some bond stretching out from her soul to his and tying them together stronger than anything but the hand of fate. Which sounded crazy. She'd known the man for a single day. A single *crazy* day.

If she was feeling anything, it was because of adrenaline. Attraction was one thing. How could she even start to contemplate a forever? No one had made her think those things before and she shouldn't be starting now.

Crazy talk.

She sank down onto the couch and curled in on herself. She felt safe enough that she started to panic as everything washed over her. What was going to happen to her? What if running ruined Michaels' case? What if she got arrested for obstructing justice?

She was in deep shit.

Kerry let the panic take her while Bryan made his calls. She didn't want him to see her like this and a distant part of her thought that letting the emotions bubble to the surface for a few minutes would be enough to flush them from her system.

By the time Bryan came back inside, she wasn't shaking, and though he gave her a searching look, he didn't say anything.

Good.

She didn't need pity.

And by the time she was ready for bed, she'd basically forgotten the panic. Bryan had a way of putting her at ease and she let him do it. She wanted him to. She just plain wanted *him*.

It was on the tip of her tongue to invite him into her room with her as she got ready for bed. The bed could fit two if they squeezed tight. Her body burned just thinking about it.

But she didn't *quite* have the nerve to do it so she told him goodnight and closed the door behind her.

Goodnight was a freaking lie.

The nightmares took her the moment she surrendered to sleep, and they refused to let her go. She finally wrenched herself awake, body covered in sweat and sheets tangled around her legs. A glance at the bedside clock told her it was just past midnight.

Not even an hour of sleep.

Damn it.

She lay back, eyes heavy but refusing to close. She could feel the nightmares lurking, ready to claw her back into the violent darkness. When the threat of the nightmare didn't let her go, Kerry sat up and planted her feet firmly on the ground. The house was chilly in the autumn night and she was glad for it, but the sweat rapidly cooling on her skin made her shiver.

With no better idea, she shuffled out of bed and headed for the kitchen to get a glass of water. And once that was in hand, she looked out at the living room and noticed Bryan sleeping on the couch.

No, not sleeping anymore. His eyes were open and he was looking right at her.

"Why aren't you in one of the bedrooms?" she asked. She felt like a poor host, even though she was most certainly the guest in this scenario. But it felt wrong to sleep in a bed when someone else was stuck with the couch.

"I'm not sleeping in Gibson's room," he said as he sat up; he must have been referring to the other bedroom on the main floor. "And all the other bedrooms are downstairs. I didn't want to be on a different floor. Just in case."

"Oh." She gripped her water and took a nervous sip. It wasn't cold enough and she wished she had ice cubes. "Do you think there's any danger here?"

He shook his head. "No, but I've messed this job up enough already. I'm not going to screw it up again."

It was the most natural thing in the world to take three steps and sit beside him on the couch. The cushions were warm from his body. "You haven't screwed it up. We're both alive."

He huffed out a sour laugh. "What happened at your apartment shouldn't have. And now we are running blind, just *hoping* we don't get shot at again. Not exactly a glowing start to the job."

"We're both alive, aren't we? I never would have made it out of my apartment without you." And she didn't want to consider what might have happened if the gunman had gotten inside. Did he just want to kill her? Or worse?

Bryan leaned back against the cushions and gave her a sleepy smile. "You should go back to sleep."

"You shouldn't be sleeping on a couch." There were plenty of beds in the house, but that wasn't what

Kerry immediately thought of. "If you won't sleep in your boss's bed, there's plenty of room for two in mine."

Bryan didn't breathe. He was frozen as if in the eyes of a predator, quite the feat considering *he* was the predator. Or, rather, they both were. They were close enough to touch, but the chasm of an inch stretched between them.

Kerry leaned her leg in just far enough to close it. "You'll sleep better in a bed. Come on." She held out her hand.

It didn't occur to her to offer to move to one of the downstairs bedrooms where they could both sleep alone. And if the thought tried to whisper her way, she quelled it.

Bryan took her hand and they stood. She led him to the bed and laid down. He joined her. And as if instinct overtook him, as soon as the covers settled over them, he slung his arm around her and held her close.

Kerry felt her muscles loosen and the last vestiges of the nightmare release her.

They both needed this.

And as she drifted off to sleep, she let herself believe that things just might turn out alright.

# CHAPTER SIXTEEN

"They're so *cute*, it's a shame to wake them." The words from a voice she didn't recognize had Kerry jolting awake, and Bryan's arm let go of her without any resistance. A man she didn't recognize stood over her bed, grinning down at them with a smile broad enough to break his face.

A brunette woman stood in the door frame, face carefully blank as she stared at the man. There was something about the woman's face that looked famil- iar. Kerry didn't think she'd ever seen her before, but she'd seen someone who looked like her.

AR Selby.

That was too weird to think about, and Kerry tried to blink the sleepy thought away. No way had AR tracked them down. No way would he need to. He worked with her father. Why would he have anything to do with the danger against her?

"Owen, I swear to god, if you're not out of here in ten seconds I will rip something important off of you." Bryan murmured it from where he lay, words muffled but clear enough to make Owen laugh.

Owen. One of his pack members. Which probably made the serious woman in the doorway Stasia.

"Don't take anything my lovely mate would miss." Owen kept laughing, standing far enough away to dodge any blows. "And get up, sleepyheads. We've got breakfast."

Bryan groaned and waved a hand at Owen, who finally left them alone.

Bryan turned onto his side and put a hand on her shoulder. "Owen's a tease, but he won't do anything worse. I'm sorry that's how you had to meet him." The sleep was clearing out of his eyes and he was so close that Kerry almost leaned in and captured his mouth.

Only the self-consciousness of her morning breath and the thought that there were two shifters waiting for them right outside kept her still.

Bryan's eyes flicked downward and he stared at her lips.

Kerry forced herself to pull away. A night in his arms was more than she could have hoped for and his presence had kept her terrible nightmares at bay. She didn't normally like sleeping beside people but Bryan was different.

*You know why*, that voice in her mind whispered.

She couldn't deal with that right now. She was sleeping in the touristy shirt that they'd bought before leaving the city and pulled on her jeans. "Do you guys keep spare clothes here? We probably need to hit up a store sooner rather than later."

"There should be some stuff. But I asked Owen and Stasia to bring some clothes and toiletries for us." She could hear him moving, throwing the rest of the covers off of himself and pulling on his shirt.

Kerry tried not to be disappointed. She hadn't gotten a good look at his chest last night, but feeling it through her own shirt had been a little slice of heaven.

One she planned to feel again. Sleeping in Bryan's arms was better than a sleeping pill and she didn't wake up feeling fuzzy.

No, she just woke up full of want.

She was fully dressed, but she waited for him to finish pulling on his shirt. She didn't know Owen or Stasia, and she wasn't sure she wanted to be alone with them.

Wait. Stasia.

"Is she the one you—" She didn't have to finish the sentence.

Bryan cut her off. "Yes."

"Okay." She wasn't sure if she was supposed to do anything with that information. Owen had seemed happy enough while he teased them, and though Stasia was serious, Kerry hadn't sensed any enmity coming from her. Perhaps she really was alright with things. She dug her hand into her purse and snatched the toothbrush and toothpaste she'd taken from her father's house. "I'm going to brush my teeth."

She darted across the hall and didn't see Owen or Stasia lurking. Good. She took her time, brushing so thoroughly she was surprised her gums weren't bleeding. She looked around the small bathroom for any face soap, but there was nothing. Instead she used the hand soap and hoped it wouldn't dry out her skin completely. She was pretty sure she had some hand lotion buried in her purse that she could use as moisturizer in a pinch.

When she'd wasted every second that she could, she took a deep breath, straightened her shoulders, and went to meet the shifters waiting in the kitchen.

Owen and Stasia were speaking quietly to one another and eating pizza. Stasia had a small smile on her face that made her look almost soft. Owen was looking at her with hearts in his eyes, and Kerry wouldn't have been surprised if he had his mate's name tattooed on his forehead.

*Mate.*

There was that word again. But she had to ignore it. They had bigger things to deal with.

"Pizza?" she asked. "For breakfast?" She'd had left-over pizza before, of course, but this one was steaming, as if it had just been picked up.

"Breakfast pizza," Owen explained. "There's only the one restaurant out here and they stay on brand. But they open early. Try some." He offered her a paper plate.

Kerry took the plate and looked at the pizza. There was cheese and eggs and bacon all on some sort of white sauce. Breakfast pizza. Okay.

"Coffee?" she asked after grabbing a slice.

"In the pot," said Stasia. "Do you take anything in it?"

"Black is fine." Before she could move to get a mug, Stasia was across the kitchen and pouring two mugs.

Owen moaned. "How can you drink it like that? It's so bitter."

"Like my soul." She accepted the mug from Stasia and the words just popped out.

Owen's mouth dropped open, and then he burst out laughing. "Okay. We can keep you."

"Who's keeping Kerry?" Bryan joined them, smelling fresh. He must have used the bathroom on the lower level. He didn't sling an arm around her or kiss her, but he stood close enough that their sides nearly brushed.

Owen looked at them and grinned. Stasia observed them with raised eyebrows.

"Just eat your breakfast," she muttered.

Eating, once they got down to it, was a silent affair. And quick. Apparently shifters didn't mess around. Bryan made his own coffee with a flavored creamer that he dug out of the back of the fridge and enough sugar to make Kerry's teeth melt.

But once the pizza was done, it was time to get down to business. Though what business they were going over, Kerry wasn't sure.

"Kerry's a werewolf," Bryan blurted out once they moved to the living room, a tablet sitting on the coffee table in front of them. She sat beside Bryan while Stasia and Owen were sitting on two swivel chairs opposite them.

"Are you going to say that out loud to everyone?" She wasn't mad, exactly, but it felt like something that she should have revealed. Of course, it might have taken her hours to get the courage.

"Shifters, not werewolves," Owen reminded him.

"How?" Stasia asked.

So Kerry went through the story again, and her mind took her back to that night. Only the feel of Bryan's body heat right next to her kept her from sinking into a panic attack.

And as she recalled the night, she realized something else.

"Holy shit, that guy was there." She'd finished summing up the bite and her run and quick capture by the cops, but that wasn't the important thing. "The guy from my dad's place..." She struggled to find his name. "AR."

"Shit." Stasia scowled.

Owen reached out and took her hand.

Huh? She looked at Bryan in question.

"AR Selby is Stasia's brother. Their father is Armand Selby. It could just be a coincidence that he was at your father's place last night, and I'm inclined to think it is. He has his fingers in a lot of pies." He reached over and grabbed the tablet. "And for the last several months, unfortunately, we've suspected that he may be tied to us. Somehow." He slid his fingers over the screen before handing it over to her.

Kerry looked at the tablet. "What am I looking at?" There were pictures of a bunch of people and names and dates.

"These people were either witches or shifters and they disappeared on the East Coast in the last few years," Stasia answered. Though there was a suggestion that her brother might be some kind of evil mastermind, her voice was steady. Maybe she was already used to the evil lurking in her family. "A few months ago, the pack helped take down a witch that was murdering other witches and stealing their power. That led us to this conspiracy. Rowe and Vi might be able to explain more, but they're on a job now and we can't call them back. We found information which may link my brother to Germany, back when most of the pack was abducted and transformed. And there's been some more circumstantial evidence since then. We have a picture of my brother with a large dog on a ski trip. Could be a husky, but it's big, and everyone in this room knows what a shifted werewolf looks like."

Kerry swiped through the images until she came to the one Stasia mentioned. It looked like it had been taken from some distance. Snow fell all around them and AR was wearing ski gear. Beside him sat a huge gray canine. And, yeah, that looked like a werewolf.

"Is he a were—a shifter?" She felt like she should be able to tell, but she hadn't recognized the wolf in Bryan, nor had he recognized her.

"Doesn't seem that way. But there's more images from that ski trip. He seems to be controlling the wolf somehow. Rowe couldn't get close enough to figure it out and Vi said the place was warded to hell and back. She couldn't send in any magical feelers. So what do you mean when you say he was there that night? He was involved with the shooting?"

Kerry hated remembering that time, even if Michaels made her go over events twelve million times, just to make sure her testimony was right. She closed her eyes to better envision the scene.

The man who'd come into the shop to pick up the package was taking cover behind his car while his driver exchanged fire with two other men. The state was trying the man who'd come into her shop. He'd been wounded and caught that night. His driver had driven away before the police could apprehend him, as had the other two men.

But there'd been a third car, one Kerry had barely noticed at the time. And a man sitting in the driver's seat. She imagined a faint glow around him and she didn't know if it was her memory or her imagination that was doing it. But she was almost certain that man was AR Selby. And that the shifter who'd attacked her had come from his direction. He was parked right in front of the entrance to a park.

The three shifters with her accepted the story. That was a relief. Michaels had seemed determined to tear it down and trip her up. She'd said it was to prepare Kerry for the witness stand, but Kerry just felt under attack.

Stasia looked at Owen and Bryan before heaving a big sigh. "I think I should talk to AR."

"What?" Bryan exclaimed.

"No!" Owen practically jumped out of his seat with the denial.

Stasia gave them a second to calm down before she continued, unabated. "He's my brother. I don't think he'll hurt me. And while I'm distracting him, Owen can sneak into his home office and clone his hard drive. We need to get information directly from him. This is the best shot." She sounded so self assured that Kerry was nodding along with her.

But Owen and Bryan weren't so sure. "Remember that time he tried to have you kidnapped?" Owen snapped.

"We don't know that was him."

"Who else could it be?" her mate demanded.

"He's made no move against me since then. He

doesn't seem to know I'm a shifter, though he might suspect. And if he tries anything, you'll be right there. This is a good plan."

"It's not."

"We have to do it."

"No, we don't." Owen gripped the arm rests of his chair tight enough that Kerry was worried they would snap off.

"You're not going to stop me from talking with my brother. Deal with it."

# CHAPTER SEVENTEEN

OWEN AND STASIA didn't stick around for much longer, and for that Bryan was thankful. Stasia refused to budge on her plan and Owen looked like he was about to pop a blood vessel from the stress of it. No doubt they'd argue more on the drive back to the city.

Bryan's money was on Stasia. She didn't back down when she wanted something. And Owen couldn't refuse her anything.

That left him and Kerry alone at the farm and as safe as they were going to get. It was a heady feeling.

"Want to go for a run?" he asked after he'd cleaned up the pizza box and plates from the kitchen.

Kerry's face brightened and she nodded. "I've always run in the city, except for yesterday. I don't get to do it often."

No doubt. Bryan didn't even try, not when he could come out to Gibson's place and run for miles without a worry. "Come on."

The door had a sensor on the inside and outside that could be activated by a wolf's paw. It meant they could shift indoors and walk outside without getting naked. Usually they shifted back to human outside, just in case their fur was covered with mud or anything else Gibson wouldn't want them tracking into the house. But no matter how desperate Bryan was to see Kerry naked, he wouldn't make her shift in the open, not until she was ready.

His beautiful wolf walked outside, her fur radiant in the sunlight. He'd shifted to his own wolf form and was laying on the grass, soaking up the late autumn warmth. He wasn't sure he even needed to run. This was its own kind of paradise. But Kerry sank low and growled in the back of her throat, the warning coming right before she nipped his flank.

Bryan bounded to his feet and flipped to face her. So that was how she wanted to play it?

He was ready when she pounced on him, teeth and claws making contact, but not hard enough to do any damage. No, this was all about play. And, he realized, she'd never been able to play in this form before. He and the others did this all the time, pouncing and clawing and nipping. It was fun, and as natural as running through the woods.

But Kerry had been completely on her own. She'd never known the simple pleasure that came from playing as a wolf.

She was surprisingly adept at it, though. She almost had him pinned and he realized he was holding back. He couldn't make himself hurt her, not even in play, not even when he *knew* that none of the nips or scratches would last more than a few minutes. They healed fast and their fur was thick. They could take a lot of damage in this form.

But he would bite his own paws off before he damaged her.

That didn't mean he was willing to lose. He still had his pride.

Bryan took off running for the woods with Kerry close on his tail. She was fast, maybe even faster than him, but she didn't know the area. And she was a city wolf. She was used to exhaust and cars and rats, not the scents of greenery and deer, and other animals of the forest.

But if she was disoriented by the new smells, she didn't show it. She kept up with him, even tackling him once and pinning him, before nipping at him and backing away.

It was on. No more Mr. Nice Wolf.

Bryan darted forward and put on as much speed as he could. He was bigger, his legs were longer, and he knew this path. Kerry didn't have a chance of keeping up, though she tried valiantly.

He snuck into a little niche between two fallen trees, a favorite ambush spot among the pack. And there he waited, his body vibrating with anticipation as he heard Kerry tear through the brush, following his path.

She stopped right in front of him, head tilted as she tried to catch his scent. But it didn't go any further. She circled around, looking for him, and then put her nose to the ground, searching even harder for his scent.

He sank back into the shadows of the niche and gave her just enough time to let those doubts grow. She knew he had to be somewhere. But the niche was well hidden, and once she'd turned fully around so her flank was to him, he pounced.

Kerry yelped in surprise and tried to flip him off of her, but there was no chance of that, not when she'd been caught so completely unaware.

They tussled again, but this time, if they were keeping score and if there was a winner, it was Bryan.

He nipped at her in triumph and though she growled, he didn't feel any threat.

He jumped off of her and they ran together through the dense trees. It was its own kind of paradise, one Bryan hadn't known he could have until he became a shifter. The simple pleasure of running with the wind in his fur almost made him wish that he had no human form.

Almost.

But he could remember the gleam of Kerry's hair in the moonlight and the wicked humor he sometimes spotted in her eyes.

There were pleasures to humanity too. Though they weren't simple at all.

They had to run back to the house eventually, though Bryan was briefly seized by the desire to turn west and keep going until they found a place that no one knew but them. But who was he kidding? They couldn't run forever.

He let them back into the house by pressing the sensor by the back door and Kerry brushed up against his fur. He wanted to lean into her, but she was gone before he could do anything more than look.

Already he wanted to go back outside and run some more. But his wolf would have to wait for another day.

He had a woman to watch.

# CHAPTER EIGHTEEN

Her skin always felt too tight when she shifted between forms. Kerry stretched her arms as wide as she could, trying to get rid of the feeling. She wasn't sure if it did anything, but moving was better than sitting still.

And right now she was full of energy. Too full. The run should have tired her out. It should have left her ready for a lazy nap in the sun.

Instead she was full of a need she couldn't name. No, that was a lie. She could name it easily. She was just afraid to admit it to herself.

She wanted.

She wanted so bad that she ached with it. It was a want that had settled into her bones not long after Bryan had first walked into her life, and it was completely nonsensical. She barely knew the guy. She *couldn't* know the guy, not after two adrenaline filled days where her life had turned upside down.

The only thing standing between them was the closed door to her room. She knew he was in the house somewhere and all she had to do was walk out and find him.

And take him.

They hadn't talked about the kiss. But she'd spent the night in his arms and slept better than she could dream.

Who needed words? They were wolves. They demanded action.

Instead, she stretched some more as she stewed.

It didn't have to mean anything. She could walk outside, find Bryan, have some fun, and call it done as soon as they finished. Or as soon as they left this house.

*Liar.*

If she couldn't convince her conscious mind, there was no way she'd convince her heart of that. Kerry wasn't a woman built for casual, especially not when the wolf that lived in the heart of her was demanding something more serious than she'd ever imagined.

*Mate.*

She shuddered at the thought, a mix of fear and

wanting swirling inside of her and leading to more confusion. What did that really mean? And how could she just *know* or think she knew? She researched things. Deliberated. Tested out her options. She'd never once looked at something and known it would be hers.

So how could Bryan Vega be different?

If her wolf was listening to her inner turmoil, it didn't deign to give a response to that. Great. Now Kerry was thinking in multiple personalities. Where would *that* lead? She didn't think they had rooms for werewolves in the mental hospital.

Bryan tapped lightly on her door and Kerry stared for a moment, her wants and needs and doubts all jumbled together.

She was being a baby. A stupid, cowardly baby. She couldn't just hide in her room all night. And she wasn't going to let fear rule her, not here. She had real reasons to fear, reasons that involved scary men with big guns. But those men weren't here right now, and she had no need to fear Bryan.

He'd never hurt her.

She opened the door and there he was. His scent wafted over her, masculine with a faint hint of pine.

"Hey." He smiled, leaning against the door frame. "Are you going to want pizza for dinner? Otherwise, there's a small shop down the street from the pizza place. I can probably find enough for dinner."

"I'm not hungry." The turmoil of the last couple of days had thrown her internal schedule completely off kilter, and Kerry wasn't sure if she'd ever want to eat again.

"Oh. Okay." He kept leaning there, not saying anything. Maybe he didn't know what to say to her.

She felt the same. But she didn't want him to go.

And when he rolled back on his heel, she shot her arm out to catch him. Their eyes met, gazes clashing, and Kerry saw the war in herself reflected in his expression. Whatever was going on, she wasn't alone.

To hell with hesitating.

Kerry stepped forward, wrapped her hand around the back of Bryan's neck, and pulled him down to kiss her.

When their lips met, everything inside of her sighed in relief. *This* was right. What she was waiting for. What she knew she needed.

He was still for a moment, as if he couldn't believe that Kerry had gone for it. But that moment didn't last for long. Thankfully.

Bryan's arms went around her, pulling her tight to him, until their bodies were flush up against one another, their clothes the only thing keeping them apart. He was no hesitant kisser and he took control, his tongue delving in and tangling with hers.

Kerry groaned against him, her legs going liquid. How was she supposed to stand when she had Bryan in her arms?

She wanted him everywhere.

In any other circumstances she might have been screaming at herself: too much, too fast. Slow down.

But this was Bryan. There was no such thing as too much.

She pulled him back towards the bed and they tumbled down onto it, her legs going around his hips, feeling the hard press of his cock against her as her own sensitive skin rasped against her jeans. It was torture. Kerry would have torn off her clothes right then if it didn't mean letting go of Bryan, of not kissing him for even a second.

Impossible.

But she wanted his skin. Her nails scraped along his shirt, but they were still human, not the wicked claws she could use in her other form. She didn't rip the shirt up, even if it was stupid and getting in her way. She let her fingers quest under it, the fabric riding up to expose his stomach, his abs, the hot skin that she wanted to feel all over her.

Bryan groaned as she explored him and every one

of his sounds made her body ignite. How hot could she burn? She had a feeling she was going to find out.

Would the flames incinerate them both?

Bryan pulled away for just a second, reaching behind his head and yanking his shirt off so swiftly she thought she heard the seams rip. That would be his problem for later. Right then Kerry was going to enjoy everything he bared to her.

Between the tightness from the shift and the heat of the moment, Kerry was about to explode and she squirmed until she could get her own top off. Bryan let out an unholy sound when he realized she hadn't been wearing a bra. She couldn't stand the confinement immediately after a shift. She'd been planning to put one on before she left the room.

Now she was glad she hadn't.

He pulled back and looked down at her, his eyes shifting from their normal color to something yellow and wolfish. Maybe she should have been nervous. But Kerry's own wolf was demanding more, and nothing in her was capable of fearing Bryan.

He was hers.

He opened his mouth for a moment before clamping it shut and holding his lips tightly together, as if trying to suppress a grin.

"What?" Kerry might have felt exposed under

other circumstances, but she liked the feel of Bryan's eyes on her. And since she couldn't tear her gaze away from him, it only seemed fair.

"I'm not about to say anything that will get me kicked out of your bed." His voice had taken on a rough undertone, as if he wasn't completely in control.

It made her shiver.

"Then use your mouth for something else."

He didn't need to be told twice. He kissed her again, before sliding down her body and worshiping her breasts. His mouth was on one of her nipples, his fingers on the other, doing wicked things that made her squirm and pant for more.

She wanted everything that he could give her. She wanted to invent new ways to take pleasure, just so they could give that much more to one another. But most of all, she wanted *this,* now, and if she didn't get it, she might go mad with want.

Bryan had moved further down her body, his fingers teasing the button of her jeans, when something pinged at the edge of her awareness. It pinged again and Bryan stiffened.

Then he pulled back and cursed.

It was a ringing phone.

He cursed again. "That's the boss. He doesn't call

if it's not important." He reached into his pants and pulled out his phone. "Please don't kill me for answering this. This could be about your case."

Kerry let herself sink into the mattress for a moment while Bryan took the call. Then she groped for her shirt and pulled it back on, quickly covering herself back up. She fled the room, even when he tried to hold her hand and keep her there.

But it was a harsh reminder. The outside world could intrude at any moment.

And she wasn't safe.

Or satisfied.

# CHAPTER NINETEEN

Kerry thought she knew the definition of sexually frustrated. She'd had her dry spells before.

She didn't realize how much worse it could be when the spell wasn't dry, it just wasn't... complete.

She could see the New York skyline in the distance as they got closer to the city, two days at the farm fading away as if they hadn't happened at all. The call from Bryan's boss hadn't had anything to do with her case, after all, but was instead a notification that one of Bryan's co-workers, Jackson, would be available if he needed help.

The smart thing to do at that point would have been to pull back. Bryan was supposed to be protecting her. Could he do that effectively if he was busy trying to get into her pants?

Unfortunately, Kerry couldn't make herself care. Not when the feel of his lips on hers was like coming home.

But his phone was a freaking torture device.

She'd tried to play it cool after Gibson called. That had lasted all of an hour. Then they'd been sitting beside one another on the couch, one thing had led to another, and his lips had been on hers and his hand in her pants in minutes.

Until his phone buzzed again.

And again the next day when he'd had her pressed up against the wall, had sunk down to his knees, and had a promise of paradise in his eyes.

Then Owen called.

Phones were the devil and if she had a time machine, she was gunning for Alexander Graham Bell.

But now they were headed back into the city to stay with Stasia and Owen while those two planned their infiltration of AR Selby's penthouse.

"I should get in touch with Michaels," she realized as she said it out loud. "She's probably going crazy ever since we ditched my phone. I guess I could have used yours to call her." But truthfully, Kerry had liked the break from the prosecutor's calls. She'd spent the last year wrapped up in this case and it had taken over her life.

Three days away, even with armed gunmen chasing them, was its own kind of vacation.

Bryan's fingers tightened on the steering wheel and his jaw ticked. Despite that, he nodded. "You're probably right. And you'll need to call Detective Harper and see if he's made any headway on the shooting. Maybe they know who's after you. I should talk to him, too."

She could tell him to detour to the police station so they could get at least part of that chore done with, but Kerry didn't suggest it. She had a feeling both Harper and Michaels would yell at her when she finally got in touch, and if she could put it off for a few more hours, she would.

Besides, it was still early in the day. She had plenty of time.

"Is Stasia really okay with us staying at her place? She understands what happened at mine?" Kerry didn't want to bring trouble to the other woman. She would have been happy to stay at the farm house forever. Or at least until she got bored of country life and pizza. But her problems weren't going to go away by ignoring them.

She wasn't sure what AR Selby had to do with the night of the shooting. Even now she was doubting her recollection. Had *he* really been the one she'd seen? Or was her mind playing tricks on her?

Either way, it didn't matter. He was shady in his own ways and he might have hurt Bryan and his pack. Kerry didn't like that at all.

AR had to be investigated to protect Bryan. So he'd be investigated.

"She'll be fine with it," Bryan assured her, reaching over and squeezing her hand. He didn't pull away. "We upped the security tenfold after everything went down last year. Now you'd need an army to get in. Two armies, really. Bulletproof windows, super high tech security system, *lasers*," he grinned big at that, "and an automatic alert to everyone in the pack if the system is triggered. Not to mention that Owen and Stasia are both shifters and are a security system in and of themselves. It's probably the safest place in the city for you. And it's super swanky. The Selby corporation's crimes have definitely paid, and Stasia isn't too conflicted about using the money in her trust fund."

Must be nice.

Kerry kept that thought to herself. But, really, did she have room to complain? Her father financed most of the gallery and she'd been taking his money her entire life. If she was living on the gallery's real income, rather than the supplement that came from distributing whatever was in those boxes for her dad, she'd be living in a shack. Or worse. Even shacks were unaffordable in Manhattan.

Bryan parked the car in a garage near Stasia's place. "I know it's difficult to keep a car in the city, but I don't think we should return it just yet. Could come in handy."

"Sure." She didn't care. Her mind was too full and she couldn't make a decision as inconsequential as whether or not to keep the car for now. She'd let Bryan handle that.

Bryan led her down the block to a beautiful white stone building. The doorman let them in with a smile and they took an ancient, though gorgeously maintained elevator to the third floor. There were only two doors in the hallway and Bryan knocked on one.

A moment later, Stasia was there, letting them in with a small smile. "Welcome. I'm glad you made it safely." She shut the door behind them and engaged an impressive set of locks.

Kerry looked around and tried not to guess how expensive this place had to be. She spotted an honest to god dining room off the hallway. Stasia had square footage to spare.

"There's two full bathrooms upstairs, if you want

to wash your faces or anything. One in the hallway, one in the master bedroom. And dump all your stuff in the guest room. We'll figure out an extra bed later. I'm pulling some food out of the oven, so meet me in the kitchen." She led them as far as the staircase and there they split off.

Upstairs, Kerry took a look at the guest room and then glanced at Bryan. "Plenty of room for two. No need for Stasia to make up another bed somewhere."

He grinned and kissed her cheek. "You know I don't sleep well on couches."

Her heart flipped and she wanted to kiss him right there, but she forced herself to behave. It was bad enough to get interrupted by phone calls. She might actually attack Stasia without meaning to if the woman interrupted them.

She and Bryan took their time, washing off the grime of travel before heading downstairs, where the smell of garlic and meat sauce was enough to make her stomach rumble.

Stasia and Owen waited there, standing close, Stasia leaning against her mate's side as he wrapped an arm around her and nuzzled her hair. It was shockingly intimate, especially the soft looks on their faces, and Kerry had to look away before she blushed.

She would have rather caught them making out.

Bryan clambered down the stairs, making enough sound to wake the dead, and Stasia and Owen parted, though Owen kept an arm around her. When Bryan entered the kitchen, he put a hand on the small of her back and Kerry liked it so much she almost stepped away to try and resist temptation.

Screw that. Temptation was awesome.

"Food's ready," said Owen, handing out plates as Stasia cut into the lasagna. And Kerry smiled in relief when she saw the size of the portions doled out. Big enough for shifter appetites. No need to hide here.

They ate in the dining room, but didn't waste time talking as they dug in. Food came first. And it went fast. Once it was done and the plates clean, Stasia summoned them to her library, an ornate room with dark paneling and red leather furniture, and held up a flash drive.

"This is what we found," Owen said, taking the drive from his mate and plugging it into a computer on the desk.

"I thought you were waiting until we got here in case you needed backup." Bryan sounded like he was edging toward the edge of anger. "What if something went wrong?"

"The opportunity presented itself," Stasia said calmly, but her tone brooked no argument. "He invited us to dinner last night." She held up a hand before Bryan could say anything more. "And that's not the first time. We've had dinner with him several times, so it's not like he invited us because he thinks something is up. He *is* still my brother. We've been making an effort to mend our relationship. Well. We were."

Owen reached out and took his mate's hand. She squeezed it back.

"What did you find?" Kerry asked. She wasn't a part of their pack. This only related to her if AR really had been there the night of the shooting, and it wasn't like they were likely to find evidence of that. But this was a mystery that needed solving.

"A lot of encrypted data. But seriously, remind me to never piss off Gibson." Owen shuddered. "He called in a favor and had it cracked before midnight. I was up all night going through files. There's a bunch of stuff that would probably greatly interest anyone doing corporate espionage, but I don't think we care about cratering the Selby corporation."

"Not today, love," Stasia said with a fond grin.

Owen continued. "But then there were some very hidden files. Very, very hidden. Data disguised behind encryption and cloaked file types. That's where we found something."

"What?" Bryan was bouncing where he stood, and Kerry felt just as nervous. Or excited. She wasn't sure which.

Owen reached over to the keyboard and pressed a few buttons and nodded towards the television on the other side of the room. It was practically a mini-movie screen. But Kerry wasn't measuring the size when the picture popped up, dark, a little grainy, and on a night she'd never forget.

She was pretty sure it came from a dashboard camera, and it didn't give a full view of the scene. AR stepped out of a dark sedan and took cover while the men down the street exchanged fire. She couldn't see herself, but she knew she was just out of frame, cowering behind a dumpster.

He was holding something cupped in his hands, but she couldn't tell what it was. There was no sound, so she didn't know if he said anything, but after a moment whatever it was started faintly glowing. He jerked to the side, as if a bullet had gotten too close, but he stayed standing.

And then a wolf came bounding out of the park. It came right up to AR, and the thing in his hands glowed brighter.

Then AR looked towards where she was hiding and the wolf took off, running right towards her.

Owen cut the video. "He drives away about five minutes later, but not before the wolf comes back to him and then runs back into the park."

"Only five minutes?" Kerry hadn't realized she'd spoken until she saw the others looking at her. She shook her head to clear her thoughts and offered what she hoped looked like a brave smile. "It felt like a lot longer. But Harper said the whole firefight took less than ten minutes. And the cops just happened to be on patrol and heard the gunshots. Lucky timing. Or unlucky, I guess, depending on your perspective."

She was babbling. She wanted to get up, run, and never stop. Every time she was reminded of that night, she relived it. And she was reminded a lot.

Would it ever be over?

Bryan pulled her closer to where he sat on the couch and wrapped his arms around her. She surrendered to his touch, letting him give her the strength she needed to keep going.

"That's not all," Owen said after she'd disentangled herself.

"What else?" Bryan asked. He sounded ready to fight, and she was sure he wanted to hunt AR down right then and give him a piece of his mind. Or his fists.

Or his claws.

Owen scrolled through the files and brought one up, though this was just a PDF, no video. But there was a picture embedded in the file, and she recognized him. "How did you know what the guy who shot at me looked like?" She was looking at the gunman from her apartment, plain as day.

"Security footage from a restaurant across the street caught a good look at him." Owen didn't mention how he'd gotten that video and Kerry didn't ask. "This man, Paolo Diaz, is not currently employed by AR or the Selby Corporation, but he's done security work for them in the past."

"Diaz?" Stasia interjected.

"Shit," Owen winced. "I knew I was forgetting something."

"What's the matter?" Kerry asked. Her brain was going to pop with this much info.

"My brother's family," Stasia explained. "He's got a lot of cousins named Diaz. Of course, it's a common name, so could just be a coincidence."

Kerry tried to parse that, but at this point her brain was having trouble keeping up. "Your brother who you just stole this information from? Why does he have cousins that you don't?"

Stasia laughed hollowly. "Short story. Dad's been married seven times. All of my siblings are half-siblings. Selby, the brother between me and AR, is Selby Diaz. Dad had an affair with an employee. Maybe Selb's involved, but he usually stays far away from family shit."

"Are you sure you weren't born into a soap opera?" Kerry's filter was offline and she couldn't care whether or not that question was offensive.

But Stasia just smiled. "I know it's messed up. I'll call Selb and try and suss things out. Instinct says that if this guy is related, it's either a coincidence or Selb doesn't know about the messed up stuff AR is doing. They don't get along."

"There are more files on security personnel not currently officially employed by AR's company," Owen said. "It wouldn't be weird if these files were on a computer in the HR department, but there's not a good reason for AR to be keeping them. Unless he's hiring off the books. And all of these guys have histories of violence—military or private contractors." He scrolled through the document too fast for Kerry to process anything but blurred images of a bunch of scary men.

"An off the books private army," said Bryan.

Owen nodded.

"Anything about Germany?" Stasia asked. "Any hints?"

The question made Owen's shoulders slump. "Not yet. But I haven't gone through everything. We have to call Gibson and tell him what we found."

They went through more of the files and Kerry's mind reeled, still trying to process what she saw.

She completely forgot about calling Michaels and giving her an update.

# CHAPTER TWENTY

Neither Stasia nor Owen—amazingly, in his case—commented when Bryan and Kerry slept in the same room. And Bryan did his best to soothe Kerry as she tried to sleep, but her body was stiff beside him for most of the night.

He might have suggested a more passionate solution to take her mind off things, but one look in her eyes was enough to know she wasn't in the mood, and nothing would be changing her mind.

So he held her close and tried to pour all of the emotions he was feeling for her into the embrace. Whether it worked or not, he didn't know. He fell asleep in the early hours of the morning and had to hope she'd snatched a few hours for herself. She was sleeping fitfully when he woke and he did his best to sneak out of bed without waking her.

Stasia and Owen weren't in the house when he went downstairs, but there was a note saying they'd be back later and that there was plenty of food.

He couldn't soothe Kerry's anxiety, but he could make her a feast. And at least that was something. He had bacon and potatoes frying on the gorgeous, outrageously expensive stove in Stasia's kitchen. He was just cracking eggs into a bowl when Kerry entered. Her hair was a bit mussed, as if she'd just run her fingers through it, and there were dark circles under her eyes.

But she smiled at him.

As long as she smiled, his heart would be okay. He'd tear apart the world to keep her happy.

But he'd keep that to himself for now. She had enough on her plate and didn't need to hear his confessions of devotion when she was still dealing with everything else.

"You can cook?" She sounded surprised, and Bryan was just a bit offended.

"Yes. Did you think I couldn't?" The last few days hadn't exactly given him the space to showcase his culinary skills, but he'd been feeding himself for most of his life and was actually pretty good at whipping up meals out of whatever he could find in a pantry.

"I plead the fifth," she said as she slid onto a stool on the other side of the kitchen island.

"You've been listening to that prosecutor too much," he teased.

Kerry laughed. "No way, she wouldn't let anyone plead the fifth if she could get away with it. Pesky Constitution. I learned *that* from *Law and Order*. Is there anything I can help with?"

Bryan poured the eggs into a pan and shook his head. "No, this will be done in just a couple of minutes. There's coffee in the pot if you want some."

That had her off the stool and across the room in a blink. She poured herself a mug and held up the carafe to him. "Do you want some?"

He nudged his own mug her way and she filled it before silently reaching into the refrigerator, finding the flavored creamer that Owen used and adding just a bit for him. He smiled as he took it.

Kerry sat back down, grasping the mug in her hands. "Is the cooking just a skill, or is there a story behind it?"

His smile slipped a little as he plated up their dishes. He turned off the burners and sat on the stool beside her. "I'm the youngest of three. And my brother and sister are a bit older than me. When I was little, my parents were busy making sure they were taken care of, going to games and practices and all that, and I was left on my own a lot. They always gave me money for pizza so I wouldn't starve. And Mom told me not to touch the stove. So it started as a bit of a rebellion. My babysitter parked herself in front of the TV all night and didn't care what I did as long as there was no blood and I didn't set anything on fire."

"How old were you?" Her eyes were wide and worried, like she could reach through time and talk some sense into his parents.

Bryan had to think for a moment and do some mental math. "Eight or so? Rick went to the Naval Academy when I was twelve and Whitney went to college the next year. My parents were parented out after that and more or less let me roam wild." Kerry didn't need to hear about the way his parents berated him for not making the football team like his brother or getting straight As like his sister. She didn't need to hear that he'd left the day he graduated high school and had only been back twice. Her dad was a mob boss. What was a bit of casual neglect in comparison?

"They should have cared more," she said fiercely. "I don't think my dad even knows my middle name. But my mom would have done anything for me. I don't know if that would have changed as I got older. I don't think so."

"When did she…"

"Killed in a shooting when I was eight. Police never caught the guy. But Dad told me I didn't have to worry about anyone coming for me. It was taken care of." She swallowed hard. "Dad was more distant after that. He'll give me all the money I could want. It comes with strings, but what doesn't? But I don't know if he actually cares or if it's just because I'm his only child." She turned to her food after that, but both of them had nearly completed their meals while they spoke.

Bryan finished his coffee while his mind worked. He hadn't meant for the morning to include vomiting out their childhood traumas. He wanted to hold Kerry close and promise her she'd never be alone again. And from the way she kept shooting glances his way, she had something to say about his own past.

But it was useless to dwell. They were both alive and together. Who cared about shitty parents?

If he had a therapist, she'd probably want him to examine that thought.

"Come on," he said as he cleared their empty plates. "You need new clothes and we need to get out of here."

"I thought we were laying low. And I still have the clothes Stasia and Owen brought when we were at the farm house." She flattened a wrinkle in the t-shirt she was wearing and looked down at her sweats. "It's fine."

"We're going shopping, not dancing in the middle of Times Square. Or if you don't want to go shopping, we can go walk in the park. But we're not staying here all day. I'm your bodyguard and I'm telling you it's safe." He believed it. Nothing indicated that they'd been followed out of the city. And he didn't mention it, but if AR was involved, there was a chance he was monitoring Stasia's place and it was better not to be there at all hours. The security system could only do so much.

But really, he wanted to take his mate on a date. And he was going to make that happen.

After another moment, Kerry smiled. "Okay. Let me go get changed."

# CHAPTER TWENTY-ONE

Her jeans were starting to feel a bit crusty, now that Kerry thought about it. She'd washed them in the tub at the farm house after finding a few spots of blood on them, and air drying them made them stiff. So a new outfit wouldn't be amiss.

And walking down the street made her feel normal, as long as she didn't consider why she couldn't go back to her apartment.

Ugh.

She'd made it two minutes without thinking about all of the threats around her.

*Stay in the moment*, she told herself. She reached out and grabbed Bryan's hand, the warmth of his palm a steady reminder that she was here with him and everything would be okay.

Maybe.

She hoped.

Then she realized that she shouldn't be holding her bodyguard's hand and hindering his ability to reach for things. She tried to let go.

Bryan shot her a quizzical look. "Problem?" He squeezed her hand before loosening his grip, but he didn't pull away.

"Don't you need your hands free in case someone comes for me?" Her eyes scanned the crowd, but there was nothing out of the ordinary.

"Ask me again when there are bags to carry."

"Oh! I see how it is." She laughed as he led her into a department store and they found their way to the women's clothing department. At first Kerry sped through the racks, certain that Bryan would tire of this trip if she took too long, even though he was the one to suggest it.

But he stood near her and looked perfectly happy to wait. He took in their surroundings, but the department wasn't very busy and they had plenty of room to themselves. He probably had some plan cooked up of how to defend her if gunmen appeared out of nowhere, but none appeared before Kerry had a stack of clothes.

"I'm going to try these on," she said, holding up the pile.

Bryan looked towards the fitting room and furrowed his brow. "Hold on," he said, and headed for them. He came back a moment later. "There's a separate stall right outside the main fitting area. Use that. I don't want you trapped in the fitting rooms if something happens."

Right. He had to think about things like that. Kerry found the stall he was talking about, a sign indicating it was for families and wheelchair users. She was neither, and felt a little guilty taking up the space, but no one was using it and she'd be quick.

Three shirts, a pair of jeans, and a little treat of a dress she couldn't resist later, and she knew what she was keeping and what she wasn't. When they went to check out, she pulled out her credit card, but Bryan shook his head and handed over a stack of cash instead.

Kerry might have argued, but she realized a credit card purchase could be tracked. And if AR's men didn't find her, the cops could.

If they were still looking.

She groaned. "I really need to call Michaels. I meant to do it yesterday, but I forgot."

Despite his earlier teasing, Bryan took the shopping bag. "Then you'll call her once we're back."

But they didn't go right back to Stasia's. They walked through the park and sat on a bench, watching ducks swim in a small pond. Then when they passed by a fountain, Bryan offered her a penny and told her to make a wish.

He was standing right next to her and smiled as he threw his own coin in. Kerry knew she should wish for safety or for the case to be resolved quickly, but looking at Bryan, all she could think about was him.

Her thoughts weren't focused as the penny flew. All that she thought was Bryan, Bryan, Bryan.

And maybe that would be enough.

She hoped.

They stopped for lunch in a bustling restaurant and Kerry felt exposed for a few minutes, until Bryan eased her mind with jokes and a story involving Owen, a goat, and cream cheese.

"This happened when you were deployed?" she asked between bouts of laughter, tears threatening to fall.

That made Bryan howl in an entirely human way. "This happened three weeks ago!"

Neither of them stopped laughing after that.

Eventually, after more time in the park, more

time *together*, they headed back for Stasia's. It was getting chilly out and the sun was beginning to set. And though they were perfectly safe walking together at dusk, it was time to get off the streets.

Owen and Stasia still weren't home, but Bryan didn't seem concerned about that, so Kerry didn't worry.

And she realized that Bryan's phone hadn't rung all day. They really were alone.

She took the bag of clothes upstairs and headed into the bathroom. There was no need to get dressed up for a night in, but Bryan hadn't seen the dress yet, and she wanted to see his reaction.

She slipped out of her clothes and left them in a bag with the rest of her dirty laundry. No doubt Stasia had a washing machine somewhere. Or maybe she was so rich that she sent her clothes out to be laundered.

Kerry checked herself out in the mirror and frowned. The wide neck of the dress exposed her bra straps. She'd noticed it at the store but hadn't cared. Now she tried to hide them, but the neck was just too wide to do it properly. She took the dress off and shimmied her straps down under her arms, but that just made the bra feel weird.

And who was she kidding? She didn't need the bra for what she planned.

She shucked off her underwear too. Just to make things clear.

Kerry put the dress back on and gave herself a grin. It was time to find her man.

That turned out to be easier than expected. Bryan was in their room, his shirt off and pants already changed from the jeans he'd walked around in all day to a pair of sweats that hung low on his hips.

Kerry's mouth went dry looking at him. For all their making out at the farm house, she'd never taken the opportunity to look her fill, even when his shirt was off and his body pressed against hers.

And what a body it was. He had the kind of muscles that made her know he meant business, even though she knew he was much stronger than he looked thanks to his shifter strength. His broad chest tapered a bit at the waist, like a swimmer, and somehow his ass made the sweats look good.

Then he turned to face her and her breath caught. Everything about him made her body tight with want, and now the dress felt too constrictive. She was tempted to tear it off and throw herself at him, seduction be damned.

But Bryan's lips pulled into a grin and his eyes

darkened with arousal as he looked her up and down. The sweats hid nothing of his body's reaction to her.

"Do you like?" she asked, barely recognizing her own voice. Her own inner wolf was howling, not to be let out, but to get closer to Bryan. *Now.*

Kerry stayed where she was. She was the one in control.

But Bryan stalked forward and she wasn't about to back away. "You planning on going somewhere?" he asked, running his finger over the shoulder strap.

She shivered and leaned into the touch. "I thought you'd like to see." The dress was short, black, and contoured tightly to her body. Perfect for a night on the town. And absolute torture when it was the only thing keeping Bryan from touching her skin.

He let his fingers trace down a seam and only strayed off the path so he could trace under her breast. The heat of his hand was a brand against her skin, but Kerry would gladly take the heat so long as he never stopped touching her.

"I like," he said, answering the question she'd forgotten she asked. His other hand smoothed down over her hip and he groaned. "Fuck."

He must have realized she'd left the underwear behind.

Kerry grinned at him and pressed her hip harder

into his hand. His fingers trailed only a few inches down until they met the hem of the dress, and she breathed in deep as he hitched it up, confirming his suspicion.

"You're going to kill me," he said, flattening his palm against her naked hip and pulling her close. And as his lips hovered over hers, he grinned. "But what a way to go."

She didn't have a second to respond, and once they were kissing, she didn't want to. Her dress rode up and she didn't care. As far as she was concerned, Bryan could rip it off of her in strips. It had more than done its job. She wasn't much of a seductress, but that dress had done the job for her.

Or maybe it was just the strength of the pull between her and Bryan.

*Mate.*

Some other time she'd let that freak her out. But not while her body was hot and pressed tight to him.

Bryan hiked her leg up and she wrapped it around his waist, fully exposing herself to him. It was vulnerable. Needy.

Hot.

And if he didn't touch her like he meant it, she was going to start begging. The need inside threatened to consume her, a conflagration she never wanted to extinguish. How was she supposed to even try when she was standing in the middle of it?

Then she wasn't standing, as he took control and laid her down on the bed, the dress up around her waist. His eyes had gone wolfishly yellow and no doubt her own were the same. But the rest of him, the important bits, were all man.

And all hers.

If a phone started ringing now, she'd crush it in her palm like it was nothing. But she didn't dare even mention the word, as if that might summon a call. And Bryan didn't seem to be thinking about phones at all.

He stood over her like a pagan god studying his sacrifice, and Kerry was happy to be his subject. As long as he touched her. She'd drag him down herself if he waited much longer.

Whether he read the need in her eyes or was feeling it himself, Bryan came down on her, but not for a kiss. At least not on her lips.

She let out a low moan as his lips found her sex, tongue sliding through her slick folds and ratcheting up the tension even more. She was already perched on the edge of orgasm from barely anything, but Bryan showed no mercy.

Good. She'd never forgive him if he did.

His hands and tongue wove a sensual spell over her and Kerry writhed under him, one hand tangled in the sheets under her, the other clutching at his hair and holding him to her. She arched up against him as his tongue twisted around her, doing wicked things she'd be dreaming about for months.

Or forever.

But this was no dream, and she wasn't ever letting Bryan go. The strength of her emotions might scare her at another time, but not when she had him in her bed, doing everything she wanted.

And more.

He slid two fingers into her, filling her up, but not enough. She wanted to be completely stuffed with him until she forgot where she ended and he began. Her body tumbled over the edge, rippling around him as orgasm rushed over her.

Bryan didn't let up.

His eyes were still yellow as he looked up from his feast, and as he crawled up her body, she could tell his inner wolf was close to the surface, a feral beast ready to conquer. Her own was the same, riding the waves of pleasure and determined to wring everything out of this moment.

Then he was sliding into her, thick and perfect, and Kerry could do nothing but hold on for the ride.

Her teeth felt sharper than they should have been and some instinct wanted her to lunge forward and bury them in Bryan, to claim him once and for all as her own.

Instead she tipped her head back and cried out, coming again as he pumped into her, calling her name and joining her in pleasure.

They were covered in sweat, breathing hard, and right where they needed to be when Kerry heard the distant ringing of Bryan's cell phone.

She burst out laughing as he groaned.

# CHAPTER TWENTY-TWO

Kerry really couldn't put this off any longer. Last night in Bryan's arms was its own stolen paradise, but if she didn't get in touch with Michaels, she really was shirking her duty.

She was starting to hate duty.

But just after breakfast, she and Bryan bid Stasia and Owen farewell and headed towards Michaels' office. The streets were crowded, and Bryan looked around for threats that she wouldn't even notice. Kerry was on edge too, and every time someone bumped into her, her wolf threatened to rear up and cause trouble.

Kerry clamped down on those instincts.

The office was bustling when they got there. Like last time, Bryan had to wait while she went back to talk to Michaels. Unlike last time, there was no suggestion that he didn't belong.

Kerry took her seat in the uncomfortable chair and braced herself for whatever Michaels had to throw at her.

It was just as bad as she feared. Anger. Threats. The prospect of five years of obstructing justice. More anger. And disappointment.

"You almost ruined this case, Ms. Delgado," Michaels finished, finally taking a deep breath.

Kerry would rather face a rampaging werewolf than make this woman angry again. At least she could fight the werewolf. All she could do here was sink into her chair and hoped the Earth swallowed her whole.

But she didn't apologize. That was sure to set the prosecutor off even more, and Kerry wanted this over with as fast as she could manage. Besides, it was Michaels' team who'd taught her to not say anything unless she was asked a direct question.

"Harper will need your statement. The investigation is ongoing and your apartment is a crime scene. You can't stay there. Do you have accommodations?" Michaels sank back into her own chair and looked through the papers on the desk while waiting for Kerry to answer.

"Yes." She almost added more, but the witness

training kicked in. Only answer what's asked, don't add more.

Michaels raised an eyebrow. She knew exactly what Kerry was doing. Then one side of her mouth quirked up in a grin. Maybe Kerry had impressed her. Just a bit.

"I need reliable contact information from you. Things are moving fast in the case. It might resolve sooner than we thought. Especially in light of some new evidence. But you're not out of the woods yet." She pushed a piece of paper towards Kerry. "Write down where I can contact you at and the address where you're staying. Then call Harper to get him off my ass. I have nothing to do with that investigation, but he's annoying."

Kerry bit her tongue to keep from smiling at that. She took the paper and filled it out. She'd purchased a burner phone from a bodega down the street from the prosecutor's office, knowing Michaels would want a number. At least that device was less likely to be traced.

But she hesitated before writing down Stasia's address. What if someone in the office was compromised? The gunmen had found her once before. Would it happen again?

"Is there a problem, Ms. Delgado?" Michaels asked while Kerry's hand hovered over the lines on the page.

Kerry scribbled down the address and shoved the paper away. Michaels was one of the good guys. She'd do her best to protect Kerry's information.

Kerry hoped.

Michaels took the paper and her eyebrows went up when she read Stasia's address. "That's a swanky location. Family home?"

Kerry stiffened. Michaels knew who Kerry's father was, but Kerry hadn't said anything about the family business. At the beginning of this ordeal, she'd taken a lawyer with her to every meeting. It was only after a stack of papers were signed and it was made clear what Kerry would and would not reveal, that she'd decided to take the meetings by herself.

So she didn't answer now. Her father was a scary man who did scary things. Things she probably wouldn't approve of if she knew the full scope. But she wasn't going to be the one to reveal his sins to the world.

"If I don't call you by next Wednesday, get in touch," continued Michaels. And that was that.

Kerry heaved herself out of the uncomfortable chair and found Bryan waiting for her right where she'd left him. He smiled when he saw her and Kerry couldn't help but smile back, her spirits lifting from one look.

Oh yeah, she had it really freaking bad.

She took Bryan's hand on the walk to the subway station and tried to pretend that everything was okay, that they were just a normal couple on a walk in the city. No gunmen. No looming court case. No werewolves.

"You alright?" Bryan asked as awareness of every problem in her life tried to wash her away.

"Just ready for this crap to be over with. Does the danger against me end once I've testified? Is AR trying to scuttle the trial? Or does this have to do with all the wolf stuff? Is it both? What if it never ends?" She kept her voice low, not wanting anyone around her to over-hear and think she was a crazy person. She had enough problems.

Bryan stopped walking and held onto her hand so she couldn't keep going. Not that she wanted to walk alone. He used his free hand to cup her cheek, eyes intense. "Hey, it's okay. I'm here. The pack is here. No matter how long this takes, I'm not walking away."

"And after?" She could barely think about the possibility of an *after*, and she barely knew Bryan. It shouldn't matter if they had to part ways. But her wolf wanted to howl with rage at the thought.

He grinned. "I'm not walking away."

She grinned back, indescribably happy despite all the shit.

They might have stayed like that all afternoon if it wasn't for pedestrians flowing past them, some making rude sounds about them blocking the sidewalk.

Right. None of that.

With renewed hope that things might turn out okay and the thing between her and Bryan really was real, they headed for Stasia's. There was more data to go through on the flash drive and hopefully they'd start to unravel the mystery of AR Selby's involvement.

But when they arrived at the house, everything was in chaos.

The doorman wasn't standing where he should have been. The lobby was empty. And there was a strange smell in the air.

She and Bryan ignored the elevator and ran up the stairs at top speed, but when they made it to Stasia's apartment, whatever had happened was done. The door hung open, frame broken. The air smelled faintly of chemical smoke.

There was a streak of blood on the wall right inside.

And that was as far as Kerry got before Bryan put an arm on her shoulder. "Behind me," he warned, voice serious. "We don't know who's still here."

She wasn't about to argue. And he needed someone to cover his back.

The kitchen was a mess, a meal strewn across the counter and the floor where a boot had crushed a whole tomato, its juices bleeding out around the broken skin. Before they went any further, Bryan held up a hand and they stopped.

He tilted his head to the side, and then Kerry heard it too.

A weak canine whine.

Kerry wanted to rush, but Bryan kept the careful pace all the way to the study, where the French doors that faced the park were blown out and it looked like a hurricane had rolled through.

A wolf lay behind the couch, blood on its fur. And not far from it was a human in a widening pool of his own blood. But the human's chest rose and fell. He wasn't dead.

Yet.

"Stasia!" Bryan rushed forward and ran his hands over her fur. "Where's Owen? Can you shift back?"

Kerry did a quick sweep of the rest of the room,

fearing she might find a fallen Owen, but it was only Stasia and the man.

Bryan grunted and Stasia yelped, and by the time Kerry's head had fully turned to look at them, Stasia was in the middle of shifting and Bryan held a wicked shard of glass in one hand. The point of it was dark red with Stasia's blood.

"Owen!" It was Stasia's first word when she had a human throat. She lunged for the injured man, but Bryan stopped her.

"What happened?" Bryan asked before shaking his head. "No time. This had to be loud. The cops will be coming." He grimaced and glanced at Kerry before reaching into his pocket and grabbing the keys to the rental car, which he tossed to her. "Be on high alert. Get the car and bring it around. We can't be delayed here."

"They took Owen," Stasia growled. Then she glared at Kerry. "They want you, but they took him."

Bryan stopped her before she could lunge again, and Kerry got out of there, running for the parking lot. She had no idea where they were supposed to go, but Bryan was right.

They had to run.

# CHAPTER TWENTY-THREE

Bryan was covered in blood by the time everything was settled at the offices in Brooklyn. He'd locked the human up in a secure room, settled Kerry and Stasia on the couches in the recreation area, and parked the car in the warehouse so it wouldn't be towed.

Internally he was freaking out, and he couldn't face Stasia and Kerry when he was about to explode with worry.

So he paced back and forth in the warehouse and pulled out his phone. The first call was easy. Gibson said Jackson was their backup. He called her and clenched the phone tight as it kept ringing.

But she picked up.

"I need you at the offices ASAP." No time for pleasantries.

And Jackson must have understood his tone. "I'll be there as soon as I can, but it'll be a few hours. I'm in New Jersey."

He didn't know why it would take her so long to cross the fucking river, but Jackson didn't make excuses and she didn't exaggerate timelines. "Someone took Owen and injured Stasia."

She swore. "I'm on my way."

The next call was to Gibson. The phone rang and rang, but the major didn't answer. Bryan tried again after ten rings. Still nothing. Not even voicemail. He couldn't put details into a text message, so instead he wrote: **EMERGENCY** and hoped that would be enough.

He wished Andre was still working with the pack on a regular basis, but he and his mate were off on a European music tour and couldn't be reached. They'd drop everything to come back if they knew, but Bryan would let Gibson make that call.

If the man would answer his phone.

The last member of their pack, Willa Hunter, was visiting family on the west coast. He called her anyway. She didn't pick up.

She would have answered Gibson's call.

He sent her a text as well: **Emergency situation, may need you back.**

She didn't immediately respond. And Bryan couldn't waste any more time.

He headed into the main part of the building and took a minute to wash the blood off his hands and face. There were clothes stashed in a closet somewhere, but he didn't waste time changing his shirt.

They'd have to question their prisoner, and that was likely to get bloody. Especially if he let Stasia have him. The good doctor would know exactly where to cut without killing the guy.

Neither Stasia nor Kerry were sitting when he entered the rec room, but Stasia looked almost normal. Her hair was a little wild, as if she'd run her fingers through it rather than a comb, and there was blood on her neck. But one look at her wouldn't reveal that her mate had been kidnapped and she was ready to burn down the world to find him.

Kerry wasn't hiding her feelings as well. She paced back and forth, and worry was written across her face when she looked at him. He wished he could take it away. He wished he could rewind this day so this had never happened.

Maybe if they hadn't left, Owen wouldn't have been taken.

Or maybe AR Selby would have gotten exactly what he wanted.

"Walk me through it," he told Stasia. He had a feeling she'd shatter if he showed her an ounce of sympathy. She was compartmentalizing hardcore, something she'd learned from being an emergency room doctor. He'd learned it in the Army. Would Kerry learn it today?

Stasia held herself taut, every muscle clenched as if she had to restrain herself from doing something extreme. "Owen and I were about to eat lunch. We were planning to eat on the balcony overlooking the park since it was so nice out. I'd disabled the alarm to allow us to open the doors. Someone threw a smoke bomb inside the library. I think there were four assailants. Owen injured the man you found beside me. I heard one of them demand to know where Kerry Delgado was. Then I was stabbed by the glass. I'd already shifted by that point, obviously. I was barely conscious while Owen fought. They overpowered him and took him. They abandoned the fourth man. I'm not sure if they thought he was dead or if they just knew they needed at least three men to restrain Owen." Her fists were clenched, her jaw tight.

But she was holding on.

"Jackson's on her way," he promised. "And I called Gibson and Hunter. They didn't answer their phones, but hopefully they check soon. We're going to get him back."

"What if—" She bit the question off.

"They captured him," he reminded her. "That means they have a reason to keep him alive." He didn't add the last bit.

They had a reason to keep him alive *for now.*

He and Stasia both knew it and there was no reason to say it.

"It doesn't make sense," Kerry broke in.

Both he and Stasia looked at her in question. Bryan wanted to gather her into his arms and promise her that all would be okay. But if he did that, *he* might be the one to break down. He wasn't on the same edge that Stasia was perched on, but it was close.

"What?" Stasia asked, and there was venom in her voice. It wasn't Kerry's fault, but Stasia couldn't be thinking clearly.

Kerry kept back several feet, as if she feared Stasia might actually attack her. "If these men work for AR, why now? Bryan and I were five feet from AR and a whole phalanx of his employees just a few days ago. If he'd tried to take me then, we wouldn't have been able to escape. Not both of us."

She was right about that. But before Bryan could even start to guess, Stasia offered up her theories.

That only made sense; she knew her brother far better than he did.

"It could be as simple as the fact he didn't expect to see you there," she said. "Or he's trying to keep his involvement with magic separate from his business dealings. He's been hiring his henchmen off the books, so maybe whatever he was doing in the Hamptons was business related. If we want a better idea, I think we all know who we have to ask." There was a gleam in her eye. She was ready to deal pain to get information.

She didn't suggest that AR might not have been the person to come after them. That would be too much of a coincidence.

"What if you and Owen tipped him off when you took the data?" They'd gotten out easily enough, but Bryan didn't know what kind of security AR had inside his house. Perhaps they'd been on surveillance footage the entire time.

"Don't tell me this is my fault," she snapped.

Kerry stepped forward. "It's not. So let's question this guy. Do you guys have a torture chamber somewhere? A dungeon? What's the setup?"

Despite the situation, Bryan huffed out a laugh, and even Stasia smiled. "I knew this place needed something," said Stasia.

"I'll suggest the upgrade to Gibson," Bryan added.

Kerry rolled her eyes at them. "Okay, no dungeon. Where then?"

Stasia had an idea. "The exam room doesn't have any windows. We can strap him to the table in there. The straps are designed to hold someone with shifter strength, so even if he's not completely human, he shouldn't get away."

"I'll set it up."

Fifteen minutes later, Bryan and Stasia were in the exam room with Kerry right outside the door. She'd wanted to be in there with them, but the room was small.

And she didn't need to see this. They would do what it took to get the answers.

Even if their prisoner had to scream them.

# CHAPTER TWENTY-FOUR

Bryan had looked a bit pale ever since he and Stasia had left the man tied up in the exam room. And Stasia didn't look as if getting information out of the man had done anything to heal the wound in her soul.

Only getting Owen back would fix that.

And they would. They had to.

Kerry wished she knew how.

Guilt washed over her. She'd brought this on this pack. They'd been pulled into the web of her problems and now they were paying for it. She should have never agreed to this protection.

But even as the guilt threatened to drown her, some other part of her mind reminded her that this wasn't just about her. Stasia's brother was mixed up in this up to his neck. All she'd done was witness a crime.

The reassurances rang hollow when she could still smell blood.

Stasia had retreated somewhere to shower off the worst of the blood, and Kerry was alone in the rec room. She didn't know where Bryan was, but his company would have been welcome right about now.

A wolf needed her mate at a time like this.

Kerry groaned and curled into the cushions. She *really* didn't have time to examine all the emotions that were swirling around in her head when it came to Bryan Vega. They were in the middle of a kidnapping crisis. Her heart didn't get to have a moment. Not yet.

She heard footsteps and perked up, hoping it was Bryan. Instead, a woman she didn't recognize walked in. She was tall and lithe, with long blonde hair and tanned skin, and she had a worried expression on her face. Her eyes narrowed when she saw Kerry.

"Who the hell are you? Where's Vega?" There was a hint of the South in her voice.

She must have been one of the other members of the pack. But Kerry couldn't remember their names. "He's around here somewhere." Her voice didn't tremble, that was good. And the woman looked serious, but not threatening. Considering Stasia had nearly attacked her earlier, things were looking up. "I'm Kerry Delgado," she added. "Bryan's…" What was she? How could she boil it down to a simple sentence? One word? "Bryan's been protecting me."

God, that made her sound weak. And completely ignored the most important parts of their relationship. Did they *have* a relationship?

Ugh! Stupid brain, questioning everything in the midst of a very precarious situation.

The woman pursed her lips and looked around the rec room. "Usually we stick close to the people we're protecting."

"She's perfectly safe in here, Jackson." Bryan slipped into the room through the door behind Jackson. He gave Kerry a reassuring smile. "This is Erin Jackson," he told Kerry. "Jackson, this is Kerry. It's been a bit of a week."

Kerry sputtered. Yeah, that was one way to put it.

But Jackson turned her attention to Bryan with narrowed eyes. "Seriously? You too? Remember when the rule used to be to *not* get involved with clients?"

Bryan lunged forward and enveloped Jackson in a warm hug, laughing the whole time. "I'm glad you're here, Jacks."

He looked over Jackson's shoulder to Kerry and grinned. Kerry smiled back. She still wasn't sure what was going on, but backup was always a good thing.

They separated, and Jackson gave Bryan a swift look up and down. "No injuries?" she asked. "What about Stasia?"

"She had some glass embedded in her, but it healed up the second I pulled it out. The goon we captured was a bit beat up, but Stasia made sure he wouldn't die. Of course, doing all that without numbing the guy wasn't pleasant, but they took her mate. He's lucky he's alive." He shuddered, most likely picturing the cruel healing.

"He's unconscious." Stasia entered the room and took a seat on one of the chairs. Her hair was still damp, and she was wearing oversize sweats and a large shirt. Kerry suspected they belonged to Owen. Bryan had mentioned something about the pack all keeping clothes in the offices just in case.

The woman had to be in turmoil. Kerry almost crossed the room to give her a hug, to offer comfort. But Stasia might shatter into a million pieces if she did that. Or she'd lash out.

Kerry wasn't that great at comfort anyway. She stayed where she was.

Jackson sat in a chair near Stasia, and Bryan joined Kerry on the couch. He could have taken the other end of it, but instead sat beside her, their legs touching. Jackson's teasing wasn't enough to deter him.

"What's the situation?" Jackson asked. "And how long should he be out for?"

Stasia breathed deep, and when she began talking, she was all business, the horror she felt for her mate packed away. "He's strapped to the table and I gave him enough sedative to knock out a shifter. His wounds were already beginning to heal when I began treating him, so I suspect he's not completely human; however, he did not heal as fast as a shifter. And he and his men were strong. That's part of why Owen and I were so surprised. We can handle four humans."

Jackson nodded. "Did he give you any information?"

Bryan answered that, and though he'd gone a little pale, his voice was steady. "His crew was after Kerry. Someone spotted Stasia and jumped the gun. He didn't know where they're taking Owen. There was a second crew in a vehicle outside ready to go. He and his team had vehicles of their own and were instructed to drive off in different directions to confuse a search. His vehicle was waiting in the same parking garage we parked the rental in."

"Is it still there?" Jackson asked.

Bryan shrugged. "Maybe. But if the team is as big

as he claims and as organized, someone may have gone back for it. I doubt there's much to find in the car. He said he rented it this morning."

"If he rented it, could we trace the credit card?" Kerry asked. She felt a bit like she was in a movie, but tried to ignore that.

Jackson looked her way and shook her head. "He probably used cash or a prepaid card. And we have a good idea where the money is coming from. If we were trying to prove this for a court, that would be the move to make. But…"

Right. No court of law could handle shifters. "Is there some kind of magical police?" Okay, that sounded stupid. Magic cops? Really?

But Bryan, Jackson, and Stasia all exchanged a silent conversation that Kerry couldn't decipher. Finally, Bryan spoke. "Shit, I don't know. Maybe? I didn't think witches existed either, but look where we are. If Vi was here, she might know, but she and Rowe are incommunicado on their own mission."

"I don't care if there are." Stasia was fierce. "AR is my brother, and he took my mate. I'm going to deal with him."

"We all are." Jackson reached over and patted her hand.

"Sounds great. Do we have a plan?" Kerry already

knew her part would be to stay safe back at headquarters. And though she wanted to be right in the heart of the fight, just to make sure Bryan stayed safe, she wasn't about to argue. She was no fighter. She could barely fire her gun.

Bryan, Stasia, and Jackson started throwing ideas at one another, using what little information the henchman had given them. Nothing sounded solid, and Kerry feared they were running headfirst into danger.

But they couldn't just leave Owen where he was.

"Okay," Bryan said after a long while. "In one hour, Stasia will make the call and we get AR out from whatever hole he's crawled into. He'll give us Owen if he thinks we're going to kill him. It'll work."

Even Kerry could hear the doubt in his voice.

"No."

One word sent a shock wave through the group and had all their heads turning towards the door. A man in his forties with close cropped hair and broad shoulders stood there. He looked like he could bench press a car, even without any shifter enhancements.

Kerry knew who this was. Gibson. The leader of the pack.

Jackson leapt out of her chair, while the rest of

them remained sitting. Gibson looked at her and gave her a faint nod. She nodded back. Then she sat.

"What's your idea, sir?" Bryan asked.

Gibson looked over at Stasia. "Call your father. Let's make this even more of a family matter."

# CHAPTER TWENTY-FIVE

IF STASIA WAS from a normal family, calling her father would have done nothing. But Bryan knew her family was rich beyond comprehension. Stasia herself was basically made of money, and she only had a trust fund. What kind of funds did an actual billionaire have?

Stasia had objected to Gibson's plan. She was certain her father knew nothing about the supernatural. He was a dyed in the wool atheist who wouldn't believe in magic if it happened right in front of him.

But Gibson was convincing, and Stasia made the call.

Twice.

Her father didn't answer.

Bryan knew it wasn't unusual. Stasia and her

father had a strained relationship and had gone years without talking before. But she was clearly wondering if the old man was dodging her calls because of something normal, or because of AR.

That left them scrambling for a new plan. Every minute Owen was in someone else's custody was a minute too long. None of them mentioned torture, but the prospect of it hung heavy in everyone's mind.

At one point Bryan reached out and took Kerry's hand. He wanted to find a safe place for her and lock her up tight. Did they still make towers to lock maidens in?

She'd probably shimmy out the window and kick him in the shins for even thinking about it.

But she didn't let go of his hand throughout the whole planning session.

No one suggested using her as bait, and Bryan was thankful. He didn't want to harm his pack, but violence simmered close to the surface, and he wasn't putting Kerry in any more danger than strictly necessary.

Once they were ready, that meant leaving her at the office. Alone.

He was supposed to be her bodyguard, supposed to keep her safe. Leaving her behind was a dereliction of his duty. But Kerry seemed completely fine with it.

"I'm not going to be any help in a fight," she assured him as she walked them to the garage. "And you all said this place is safe. No one knows it's connected to your pack. And I'll run if there's anything fishy."

They were bringing AR's henchman with them; he was already in the trunk of their vehicle. Best case scenario, this would be a simple prisoner exchange.

Bryan wasn't that optimistic.

Especially since they were meeting AR on his own turf. He'd sent Stasia an address and told her to come alone.

That wasn't happening.

They piled into the vehicle. Jackson had gone ahead to scout the area and set some things up. They were working on the fly, but she was a creative thinker.

It took them nearly an hour to get to AR's address. It was an old house in a shitty neighborhood. Lights were out in the houses around it, and judging by the roofs of two of those properties, they were abandoned.

Bryan hoped so. He didn't want collateral damage.

And now came the worst part of the mission.

"I've got this," Stasia assured him. She was in the driver's seat while he and Gibson were crouched down in back, a blanket thrown over them just in case anyone was watching the car. It wouldn't do much to hide them, but they hadn't wanted to risk multiple vehicles.

"Don't go into the house until everything's ready," Gibson warned.

"Not unless they drag me." Everyone knew a threat to Owen would have her running inside, but there was no way to stop that. Gibson let her go without another word.

Once she'd had a few minutes' head start, he and Gibson slid out of the back seat and into the shadows of one of the houses. It felt like they were a million miles away from Manhattan out here, in some post-apocalyptic wreck of a city. But only a couple blocks away a neighborhood was thriving and a subway would take them right into the heart of the city.

That was New York for you.

Bryan's pulse pounded and he wanted to run. His wolf was antsy under his skin and it took more concentration than usual to keep his human skin on. He and Kerry would need to go back to the farmhouse when this was all over. They'd run for hours.

But right now, he needed his head in the game.

They had no way to communicate with Stasia or Jackson. Cell phones were risky and the ear pieces they used on some jobs were bulky and relied on easily hacked radio waves.

That was fine. It had to be. This job was risky, but simple. Cause chaos and get Owen.

After several more minutes had passed, he and Gibson were forced to conclude that AR hadn't accepted the prisoner exchange. If he had, they would have come for the man already.

A flare went up.

"We're on," said Gibson, pushing off the wall and moving through the shadows like he was born to them.

The flare was the warning. Then a blast rocked a house down the street, loud enough to cause a distraction, but less damaging than the sound suggested.

Illegal fireworks were like that sometimes.

In the military they'd had access to all the explosives their hearts desired. And while Gibson had plenty of connections, even he needed a bit of time to put things together. The fireworks were a last resort, something they'd started stockpiling as half of a joke.

No one was laughing now.

He and Gibson advanced, the major in the lead. Outside the rundown house, men with guns were scanning for threats, not flinching at each new barrage of explosions. Then one yelped, and that had the others reacting.

A second one fell to the ground.

He wasn't dead, but non-lethal rounds could hurt like a motherfucker. Bryan didn't scan the nearby roofs for Jackson, but she was no doubt somewhere close, covering them and setting off the fireworks with a remote detonator. She'd only had a handful of minutes to set everything up, but she was creative like that.

It meant they only had a handful of minutes to get in, find Owen, retrieve Stasia, and get out.

If this ended with both Stasia and Owen held captive, Bryan would never forgive himself.

But he rejected the thought. They couldn't consider defeat. Not if they wanted to win.

With the men on the ground distracted, he and Gibson hurried down the dark alley on the side of the house and around the back. They jumped the fence into the yard where no one seemed to be watching the back door.

"Most likely alarmed," Gibson warned.

"Yeah." That wouldn't stop them.

They went in. The door didn't blare a siren, but it could have sent a signal to someone deeper inside the house. Inside his skin, his wolf grinned, ready for the threat.

Bring it on.

"I never meant for this to happen to you," he heard AR say from the front part of the house. "Help me and we can figure out how to fix you."

"I'm not broken, what the fuck?" That was Stasia, and he'd never heard her so angry. "What are you doing, AR? You're a businessman, why are you dealing in magic?"

"Because the business needs to grow, and I'm leaving no stone unturned."

Bryan scowled at that. He might be new to the world of magic, but he knew that they didn't need corporations getting their dirty hands on any part of it.

He and Gibson exchanged hand signals, deciding where to venture next. Getting to the staircase meant crossing in front of the room Stasia and her brother were standing in.

Their decision was made when a growl came from behind them.

Bryan turned as the shifted wolf launched itself at him. In his human form, he was more vulnerable to teeth and claws, weaker too. His gun was holstered, but he grabbed his knife between breaths and fought back, even as wolfish teeth tried to tear through his leather jacket and into his flesh.

Gibson swore, unable to get a shot while Bryan was tangled with the wolf.

The wolf barreled into him again and they crashed through a flimsy door into the room where Stasia and AR were speaking.

Bryan got his knife to the wolf's throat, ready to dig in, when his hand froze. The wolf was just as still, and out of the corner of his eye, Bryan saw something glowing.

He yanked at his hand and moved it less than an inch.

He heard a word he couldn't comprehend and froze again. What was going on? Was AR a witch? Witches had the ability to freeze people with a single thought, but it required a lot of power and a magic circle.

The spell, or whatever it was, slipped enough that Bryan could tilt his head to look to AR. Stasia had her hand wrapped around his throat, claws peeking out of her fingers. Gibson's gun was pointed at the man's head.

"Call off your dog and let him go," Stasia said in the same tone she'd used to issue orders in the ER. When AR didn't act fast enough, she squeezed.

The glow in AR's hand died and Bryan collapsed to the floor, his body suddenly his own again. The wolf yelped and ran deeper into the house.

"You will give me Owen and we will leave. No one needs to get hurt." Gibson was supposed to be the one negotiating, but Stasia was doing pretty well for herself, and neither of them stopped her.

"This isn't you, Stasia," AR pleaded, the sound choked through his constricted throat. "Let me help you."

He gagged and coughed as Stasia silently held him. Seconds passed. Finally, something in AR broke. "Upstairs. Second room."

All four of them went. There was no way they were leaving AR alone with Stasia, and it was too risky to send a person alone to recover Owen. They were halfway up the stairs when they heard the shouts.

Stasia let out a pained cry, but she was still dragging her brother with them. She looked back at Gibson, and he took AR without complaint. Stasia bounded up the rest of the stairs, Bryan close behind her. They busted through the lock on the door rather than waste time looking for a key.

And there was Owen. Stasia ran towards him and clutched him close. Most of his injuries seemed to have healed, but he was stark naked, a reminder that he'd been taken in his shifted form.

Bryan's jacket was long enough to cover the important stuff. He slipped out of it and handed it over to Owen once he and Stasia separated.

"His men will be coming in soon," Bryan said, nodding to AR. "We need to get out of here."

Owen growled low in his throat, more angry and serious than Bryan had ever seen him. He stalked towards AR, who Gibson held tight to prevent him from moving. Bryan was looking for that weird glow, but there was nothing in AR's hand.

Owen punched him, and the man slumped in Gibson's arms.

"Check his hand," Bryan said. "He was holding something."

Stasia approached her brother and examined both of his hands. His fingers were slack in unconsciousness. One of his palms was scarred, and he wasn't holding anything. Before they could do anything else, they heard a commotion from the front door.

"We need to leave," said Gibson.

They hauled ass. But when they got to the front door, it was to find Jackson waiting, eyes bright with adrenaline. "Come on, they won't be distracted for long."

They followed her to the car, taking just enough time to dump the body out of the trunk. AR or his men would find him. Eventually.

This time Gibson took the wheel, the rest of them squeezed into their seats. They took off, and Bryan hoped they hadn't just made everything worse.

# CHAPTER TWENTY-SIX

In the early hours of the morning, the crew came roaring back to the warehouse, Owen in tow. Kerry sagged in relief when she spotted Bryan. She threw herself into his arms, uncaring that everyone was looking at them, and he hugged her back, arms braced tight around her.

That was all she had the energy to do. She was asleep on her feet, anxiety the only thing keeping her awake for the past two hours.

Bryan led her up to a small office that had been converted to a bedroom, gave her a kiss, and promised to join her as soon as he took a quick shower.

Then next thing she knew she was waking up alone. The sheets beside her were warm and the mattress held the memory of Bryan's body. So where was he?

There was no clock or window in the makeshift room, and it was nearly pitch black until Kerry stumbled around and found a light switch. She winced as the light hit her sensitive eyes, but at least she could see.

Clothes in her size lay on the foot of the bed and she changed into them before venturing out into the rest of the office. Outside she heard traffic noises, and they obscured the subtler sounds from inside the office. But it didn't take her long to find the kitchen area, where Gibson and Jackson were eating breakfast. They sat on opposite sides of the large table and ate quickly. But at one point, Gibson paused and looked over at Jackson, gaze darting away before she could catch him. Jackson finished her meal, but she paused before getting up, looking over at Gibson. Then she gave her head a little shake and left the table.

Okay.

"You can come in, Ms. Delgado," Gibson bid her once Jackson had left.

Caught, Kerry entered. She'd rather flee and find Bryan, but Gibson had the kind of aura around him that was hard to resist. Was that a shifter thing or a military thing? Maybe both. Woman and wolf bristled a bit at the thought of being commanded. She'd never been the military type.

Gibson nodded towards one of the chairs, but Kerry stalled for a moment, grabbing a granola bar from a box on the counter. She would have liked something more substantial, but had a feeling that Gibson would make it a *thing* if she paused to make an omelet.

That would, she conceded mentally, be a bit of a dick move.

She took a seat at the table and unwrapped the granola bar.

"You've survived as a shifter for a year with no support. That's impressive," he said, eyes assessing her.

As a threat? An ally? A bug? Kerry wasn't sure, but she kept her mouth shut. She'd been dealing with powerful men trying to intimidate her for her entire life, and she wasn't going to bow under the pressure of Jericho Gibson.

Though she didn't know if he was trying to intimidate her. Maybe this was what he was like all the time.

"Is this the part where you tell me I have to join your pack if I want to stay in the city?" She'd managed well enough for her lonely year, but she didn't really want to be alone anymore. Especially not now that she'd found Bryan, whatever they were.

But if Gibson made some kind of threat, tried to force her hand, she couldn't join his little group. A girl had to have boundaries.

He smiled at her and suddenly looked ten years younger and whole lot more approachable. Jackson wouldn't stand a chance if this man ever shot a grin her way. "I'm hardly egotistical enough to claim all of New York for my own. Perhaps I'm not doing this shifter thing correctly, but I'm not here to viciously defend a territory. The others and I started together out of necessity. You know the story?"

She nodded, remembering Bryan's tale of kidnapping and wizards. It still seemed crazy, but she was a shifter, so how could she dispute it?

"But we've become a family over the years. We defend and protect each other. And if you want to be a part of that, you're welcome to join us." He took a sip of his coffee, eyes never leaving her face.

"And does that offer stand if Bryan and I... don't work out?" She'd almost said *break up*, but she wasn't sure if what they were doing was actually dating or if they were just falling into bed together to relieve the tension of all the danger surrounding them.

*Liar.*

Okay. So her wolf was pretty sure that she knew exactly who Bryan was to her, but that was a problem for later.

"Do you think that's going to be an issue?" he asked steadily.

"We've known each other a week." She was deflecting. But she had to. The truth was a scary thing to contemplate. How could she be thinking about forever when she'd had the carton of milk in her fridge for longer than she'd known Bryan Vega?

Thankfully, Gibson let it drop. "The offer stands, even without Vega."

"And what do I have to do to be part of this pack of yours?" Yes, she wanted community, but she didn't want strings. "I'm not exactly bodyguard material."

He smiled again with a nod. "That's true. There aren't any specific requirements. We're a family. We help one another when it's needed. We care for one another. We've been doing this for barely longer than you have. Perhaps I'm breaking some ancient shifter code, but right now I'm doing what feels right."

"So you'd be my, what, alpha? Commanding officer? Da—" Nope, she couldn't even get the last word out without a grimace.

Gibson actually laughed. "We're not big on labels

around here, not anymore." He gathered his plate and stood. "Welcome to the family."

He left her alone, and she realized that he'd welcomed her even though she hadn't technically agreed to be a part of his crew. Was she bound by that? Was there some secret werewolf code that she'd break if she walked away?

She absently ate her granola bar while she thought, but it was long gone before she came to any sort of decision.

She left the kitchen and there was Bryan. A smile eclipsed his face when he saw her, and she wrapped her arms around him. She didn't know how he could feel like home after just a week, but she never wanted to let him go.

And when she took his hand and led him back up to the room they'd shared, he followed eagerly.

"Good morning," he said, once they were behind the closed door. He pulled her close again and brushed his lips against her forehead.

She sighed against him. *This* was what it was all about. "Did you put Gibson up to that?" Just because the man said that her place in the pack wasn't dependent on Bryan, didn't mean Bryan hadn't said anything.

"Up to what?" His hand trailed up and down her back.

Kerry needed a second to remember what they were talking about. When his hands were on her, she couldn't think. But she never wanted him to stop touching her.

"Gibson invited me to join your pack. Or family. Whatever you call it." She hadn't been looking for a family. She hadn't thought she needed a pack. But the idea of a whole group of shifters backing her up made her feel safe in a way she'd never contemplated before. Yes, her father commanded plenty of violent people who'd be more than willing to kill for her. But for the right price, they'd turn those guns on Kerry.

The pack wasn't like that. *Family* didn't do that.

Bryan's hand stopped moving, and his eyes widened. "I didn't say anything." He opened his mouth but closed it before he asked any questions.

"He said I can stay whether or not we're..." She gulped, still unsure of the right word.

Bryan's eyes flashed their wolfish yellow, and his voice had a hint of a growl in it when he spoke. "We're together." He said it like a vow.

It would be wise to step back right then. Consider the relationship and what she really wanted. She'd been moving non-stop for the past week and her only constant was Bryan's steady presence. He'd burrowed his way into her body and her heart and extracting him would tear her to pieces.

If it was even possible.

But she didn't have to.

He loomed over her, eyes glowing and staring at her like she was the key to some puzzle he'd been trying to solve for ages. The pieces slid together and fit perfectly.

She wasn't walking away from this.

Ever.

She lunged for him, their mouths coming together in an almost too hard press of lips that edged into pain but had her wolf begging for more.

*Mate*, it demanded. Mate it would have.

They stumbled back to the bed, clothes flying in a rush to get skin to skin. Something feral demanded she move as fast as she could, take what she wanted, and glory in it.

That sounded fucking amazing.

Whatever control she had snapped, and she clawed down Bryan's side, getting rid of his underwear until he was completely naked under her, cock proudly jutting out and waiting for her to take it.

Her eyes had to be glowing just as brightly as his

were. Both of their wolves were riding close to the surface, and still she needed more.

She took him in hand, stroking until he groaned, and his hips thrust up against her in helpless surrender. A smile bloomed on her lips as she heard the noises he made. All for her.

All hers.

But still not close enough.

"Need to taste you," Bryan ground out, holding onto his own control by the barest thread.

All Kerry needed to do was snap it and let it take them both.

Instead, she climbed over him until she was straddling his face, her hands on the wall behind the bed while he held her thighs.

And when his lips found her, she tried to hold back the scream that threatened to rip out of her throat. This moment was stolen just for her and Bryan. She didn't need the others to hear.

But as he worked her over with his tongue, showing no mercy until she was a writhing mess who could barely hold herself up, she forgot about her fears and urged him on, begging for more, uncaring of who heard.

Orgasm swept through her, and as her body shivered, Bryan used it to his advantage, flipping their positions until he was perched on top of her, that achingly hard cock of his teasing her entrance.

He kissed her, and she could taste herself on his lips, a filthy reminder of all the things he could do to her.

With her.

He slid inside and she surrendered to it, the thrust of his flesh a welcome invasion. Forget every problem they had. They were staying in this bed for the rest of forever.

And when wildness caught them, they moved together as they chased pleasure.

It should have been enough. She was already sensitive and ready to tip over again. But she needed... more. Her mouth felt too full, her teeth too big. But she was a werewolf, not a freaking vampire.

Bryan had fangs of his own, his mouth strangely elongated as if he was in the middle of a shift, but no other part of him changed.

Their eyes locked, bodies still moving together as time slowed around them.

"Need," Bryan groaned, the word strange around his fangs. "Claim."

"Yes." *That* was it, even if her human mind didn't know exactly what it meant. Or it didn't until Bryan clamped those jaws down on her shoulder and bit.

It should have been painful, but pleasure ripped through her, sending Kerry tumbling into another orgasm. And once she had her breath back, she reared up and gave Bryan a bite of his own.

He cried out and emptied into her.

The teeth shifted back to normal, but Kerry's rapid heartbeat didn't calm. She reached up and touched the bite, her hands coming away with less blood than she would have expected.

Bryan wore a similar mark on his own shoulder. And her heart felt light when she saw it.

Whatever they were doing together, they were definitely in it deeper now.

# CHAPTER TWENTY-SEVEN

THEY GOT a couple of knowing smiles when they left the bedroom, but Kerry didn't care. She wanted to spend every minute that she could with Bryan. Some part of her insisted that those minutes were numbered.

The mate marks on their shoulder said otherwise.

She didn't know if it was shifter marriage or whatever, and she didn't care. She smiled whenever she spotted the swiftly forming scar on Bryan's shoulder. It was the only wound she'd ever *like* seeing on his body. Otherwise she never wanted him to hurt.

"You ready?" he asked. He was in bodyguard mode this morning, wearing jeans and a dark shirt with a leather jacket over it all. He looked like he meant business.

She finished buttoning her blouse and adjusted it until it fit right. Jackson had gone out and bought her an appropriate outfit to wear to the trial. It wasn't exactly Kerry's style—she didn't normally wear fuchsia because of her red hair—but it didn't look terrible. Especially not when she pulled her hair back and kept it in place with a black headband.

"I can't wait for this trial to be over." Michaels promised they'd have a court date soon, and she said this trial was moving faster than many criminal cases did. Kerry still wanted it done. Her life had been on hold for a year. She was ready for it to start again.

Bryan stepped close and kissed her quickly, pulling away before she had time to savor the taste of him.

Probably for the best. They were in range of the bed and it wouldn't take much to tip them back into it.

"Let's go," she said.

They passed by the kitchen, where the others in the pack were huddled around the table and discussing AR Selby. Kerry felt guilty for taking Bryan away from that investigation. Of course, AR also had something to do with turning her into a werewolf and possibly had some strange power to control wolves.

She'd help out once they were back, she vowed to

herself. Maybe fresh eyes would be just what the pack needed. And since she was one of them now, she wanted to be useful.

The ride to Michaels' office was uneventful. The subway wasn't even that crowded considering the time of day. As they came out of the stop, Kerry let herself believe that things might actually be okay.

That thought lasted for ten seconds.

Then half a dozen cops surrounded them, guns out and demanding that they freeze.

Her hands went up as she did exactly what they said. She prayed that Bryan didn't have a gun with him. That would turn this ugly. Slowly, Bryan's own hands went up, his eyes taking in the cops he could see.

"What's the problem, officers?" he asked calmly. He breathed shallowly, and it appeared that he wasn't moving at all.

Pedestrians were making a wide berth around them, though a few had their cameras out, filming the interaction as it went down. Kerry hoped that would keep these cops on her best behavior, but she'd seen enough videos online to know that spectators didn't ensure good behavior.

Neither did complying.

But running would be worse.

The cops ignored Bryan's question. One took handcuffs from his belt and stood in front of her, clamping the handcuffs over one wrist, jerking her hand behind her, and wrenching her other arm down until she was cuffed. "Kerry Delgado, you are under arrest."

Her mind went numb, and her perception went fuzzy as he said more. *She* was under arrest? For what?

Her first instinct was to struggle, but with guns already drawn, she couldn't risk it. She and Bryan would survive a shooting, but that would only raise more questions. And the street around them was crowded enough that bystanders might get shot. And they didn't have super shifter healing.

Bryan was demanding answers, but the cops kept ignoring him as they shuffled her off to a waiting unmarked vehicle. The only hint it was actually a cop car was the flimsy red light sitting on the dash and swirling wildly.

"Call my lawyer," she yelled at Bryan as they put her in the car. She wanted to say more, but they shoved her inside and slammed the door before she could.

It didn't look like a cop car on the inside, either. Kerry's instincts were screaming at her that something was wrong.

Of course it was wrong. She'd been arrested! But, she supposed, anyone could be arrested. There were tons of laws out there and she could have broken any one of them. She hadn't heard what they were arresting her for, her brain too distracted. Or maybe they hadn't said it at all. It didn't matter. She had a lawyer who was more shark than man, and he loved tearing criminal prosecutions apart.

She gasped in pain as the thought washed over her. Criminal prosecution. Her? She was no criminal.

And, oh god, Michaels was going to kill her when she found out.

But Kerry couldn't care about Michaels right now. She had to hope that Bryan wasn't planning to do something stupid like mount a rescue at the police station. They'd have to run forever if he pulled her out of custody.

No. She'd told him to call her lawyer. Gibson would also tell him to call her lawyer. It would be fine.

Something was *off*, though. Only two of the cops had gotten into the vehicle with her, but that was probably normal. It wasn't like one was going to ride in the back beside her. They hadn't bothered to buckle her seat belt, but maybe that was normal too. If they tried to ticket her for riding without a seat belt, she'd be pissed, though.

There were handles on the back doors.

Under normal circumstances, she wouldn't even notice that. But Kerry knew enough about cop cars to know that they didn't usually want prisoners opening the door and getting out. She didn't try it, though. She wasn't going to add resisting arrest to her charges.

Besides, angling herself towards the handle was nearly impossible with the way she was sitting on her hands. Her shoulders protested, but it was just uncomfortable. Not painful.

Yet.

Neither of the cops were talking to one another. And there wasn't anything dividing the front seat from the back seat. Shouldn't there be?

Maybe unmarked vehicles were different.

Maybe she was latching onto things that would somehow make this less real.

Maybe if she closed her eyes and wished really hard, she'd wake up in Bryan's arms and this would all turn out to be a nightmare.

No luck.

She didn't know where the nearest police station was, and the road was crowded with cars. But after they'd been weaving through traffic for at least forty-five minutes, Kerry was sure something else was up.

They were in Manhattan, surely they'd passed a police station by now.

They pulled into an underground parking garage, and Kerry *knew* something was up.

If they were near a police station, there would have been cop cars parked all around. Instead, the level they stopped on was deserted except for one other vehicle, a large industrial van that had seen better days.

A kidnapper's van.

She struggled against her handcuffs, but they wouldn't budge. The two alleged cops ignored her as they got out of the vehicle and went to the van.

She jerked her body around until she could get her hands on the door handle, but even though she pulled on it, the door didn't budge.

Child safety locks.

She hadn't managed to come up with another plan of escape when one of the cops opened the door and grabbed her feet, yanking her out while she struggled. The other one was outside the door, gun drawn.

"Try anything and we'll put you down," he said, voice dripping with bile.

Kerry stopped struggling. That cop *wanted* to shoot her. She wasn't going to give him an excuse.

She heard footsteps, and then a hulking, bald man

she recognized stepped from behind the open back doors of the van.

He worked for AR. He'd been the same man Bryan and the others decided to dump back with AR rather than keep imprisoned. Bad decision.

He scowled at her and then at the cops. "I wanted you to bring the guy."

"We had our orders," the one with the gun said. "Now take her so we can split. We don't need our sergeant noticing we're gone."

So they really were cops. Wonderful. Calling 911 would be useless if she didn't know how many of the boys in blue would return her right back to her kidnapper.

She could run. The parking garage was big, but she was fast. Maybe not outrun a bullet fast, but allegedly she could get shot and shake it off.

But what if they had silver? She remembered Bryan's story of getting shot with silver. She might not survive a silver bullet. And the asshole in the van knew about werewolves.

"Walk to him slowly," the cop with the gun instructed.

She didn't want to. She wanted to stand in place until they hauled her the ten feet to the van. If they were kidnapping her, they had to work for it.

But the cop's finger was resting on his trigger, and he was just waiting for an excuse.

Kerry walked to the van. The bald man yanked her into it, clipped her handcuffs to a chain he already had waiting in the back, and then shackled her feet. To top it off, he yanked a dark bag over her head so she couldn't see anything.

She struggled against her bonds, but it did nothing. This man knew how to tie a person up.

A short time later, the van started, and Kerry was hopeless to figure out where they were going.

Bryan would come for her. She knew he would.

She just had to survive long enough for him to find her.

# CHAPTER TWENTY-EIGHT

Bryan was going to kill someone. Rage had been beating at him since he'd watched the cops drive away with Kerry and hadn't done anything to help. Two squad cars and an unmarked vehicle were enough to cut through traffic without any issues. He'd watched until one of the squad cars and the unmarked vehicle had turned a corner and disappeared from sight.

His first move was to report it to Gibson. Gibson had some friends on the force, including the detective who'd been working with Kerry for the upcoming prosecution.

Why hadn't Harper said anything?

That was the first thing his instincts had snagged on as wrong.

What had she been arrested for?

That was the second. The cop who'd cuffed her hadn't given a charge. Maybe he didn't have to. Kerry's lawyer would deal with that issue.

And why the unmarked vehicle?

Maybe it all made sense to the cops, but to Bryan it was a mystery, and he'd tear it apart thread by thread to solve it.

No way were they keeping Kerry.

She'd given him her lawyer's number just in case something happened and Bryan made the call. He got an answering service and he left a message, internally cursing the whole time.

His phone beeped with an incoming text from Gibson. **Get back to base.**

It was the last thing Bryan wanted to do. He had to chase after Kerry and find where they'd taken her. He had to stop them before they ever put her in a cell. She didn't deserve that, and he didn't want her to go through it.

There were a hundred excuses he could give the major. Instead, Bryan confirmed his receipt of the message and headed back into the subway to catch a train back to Brooklyn.

The entire way there he plotted, though most of it was useless fantasy. Not even Gibson had the resources to lay a full assault on a police station, and definitely not in a matter of hours.

Once he was out of the station, he called Kerry's lawyer again, and this time he connected with a harried sounding secretary. He gave her a short summary of what happened and the secretary promised she'd have her attorney on it in no time.

It didn't make Bryan breathe easier. He was a soldier. A shifter. A man of action. He didn't want to sit around and make phone calls while his mate was sitting in a cell for some bullshit crime she hadn't committed.

His wolf paced under his skin, but wasn't trying to take control yet. While it wanted to fight as well, it understood that right then they didn't have anyone to fight.

Bryan was going to change that.

Everyone was waiting when he walked in, gathered around the kitchen table with laptops set up and phones going.

Gibson nodded at him when he spotted him. "I'm calling every friend I have on the force and trying to figure out where they took her and why. Jackson is working on the traffic camera footage that we can tap into, and Owen has called Harper to see if the detective had anything to do with this. Stasia is going through the files she took from her brother."

"We can tap traffic cameras?" It wasn't the most important thing, but it sounded like something out of a TV show. He knew Gibson had connections, but that seemed extreme.

Extreme was good when it came to getting Kerry back.

Jackson looked up from her monitor for a moment. "It's easier than you think. The live feeds are available in a bunch of places. Just about any camera with an internet connection can be hacked. Seriously, cover your web cam lens if you don't want everything you do to be observed." She shuddered and went back to the computer.

He filed that disturbing piece of information away. "What can I do?"

"Walk me through it." He and Gibson sat at the counter, far enough from the others so they wouldn't disturb them, but close enough that everyone would hear the story. Good. Bryan didn't want to tell it a million times.

He went through it as thoroughly as he could. And then he did it again when Gibson asked. And again.

"Six officers to arrest one woman?" Gibson mused

when Bryan broke to take a drink of water. "That's excessive even for the NYPD."

Bryan had to agree. "Unless they knew we were shifters. At this point, I wouldn't be shocked if there's some secret shifter police embedded in law enforcement."

"Vi probably would have said something," Owen offered from the table.

Rowe's mate, the witch Vi, was their main source of information when it came to the supernatural. She hadn't held anything back once she'd become a part of the pack, but she also assumed at times that they knew more than they did.

"I haven't heard a peep about shifter cops," Gibson said. "And I'd know. Let's assume they thought she was a normal woman." He paused for a long moment before speaking more carefully. "Is it possible that Kerry's father had something to do with this?"

"You think he had her arrested? Fucking bastard." He'd hunt the man down himself, crime boss resources be damned.

But Gibson was shaking his head. "I'm asking if he might have paid off some friends on the force to get her out of town. He's distantly connected to this trial that Kerry is testifying in. If she disappears, the case falls apart. And, from what I understand, he would go to some lengths to keep her safe."

The denial was right on his tongue, but Bryan forced himself to consider it, no matter how much it made him want to rage. He and Kerry hadn't spoken much about her father after leaving his house. And she hadn't mentioned getting in contact with him. "If he's involved," he finally said, "she didn't know about it. She was terrified getting into that SUV and she told me to call her lawyer. If she knew it was her dad, I think she would have said something else. Or the lawyer would have been prepared."

"Putting her in the SUV is strange, and it doesn't fit. Why not use one of the properly outfitted cop cars that was right there?" Gibson was asking rhetorically so Bryan didn't attempt to answer. "She hasn't been booked anywhere yet. I'll know as soon as she is."

But the longer this went on, the more worried Bryan grew. Something was up with the arrest. If it had to do with the shooting, Harper would have been involved, and Gibson had been in touch. The detective hadn't ordered the arrest. Unless Kerry was hiding a life of crime from him, there was no reason to arrest her.

And she didn't have the attitude of a criminal. She left that to her father.

"Give me something to do," he begged of Gibson. "Otherwise I'm going to start roaming the streets looking for her." He needed to *move*, and if he didn't burn off some of the nervous energy by doing something, he feared he would explode.

"Go help Stasia. If Kerry wasn't arrested, there's a chance AR has her. We'll need as much information as we can to deal with that. Be thorough. We'll find her."

Bryan hoped so. Because if she wasn't back in his arms soon, he'd tear the city down brick by brick to find her.

# CHAPTER TWENTY-NINE



This freaking sucked.

Kerry rolled onto her side and tried not to puke. Her stomach roiled and threatened to mutiny. She wasn't in the van anymore, but the world wouldn't stop moving. Her kidnapper had jabbed a syringe into her arm before pulling her out of the van, and everything had gone hazy.

She didn't like hazy. And she didn't think drugs were supposed to feel this way. No way would people pay thousands of dollars for a high like this.

Her stomach lost the battle and she puked.

Kerry groaned and winced at the acidic smell. But her head was starting to clear, the fuzz fading.

She forced herself back into a sitting position and

tried to ignore the sweat streaming down her face. She no longer had the bag over her head, but the room she was in was dimly lit. It looked more like a bedroom than an office, but there were no furnishings. There was a window on the opposite wall, but all she could see were the tops of a few buildings and the night sky.

Night? Oh hell. How long had she been out?

She was still handcuffed and her feet were manacled, but she wasn't chained to anything. She dragged herself to the window, inch by agonizing inch, and peered out. The buildings were familiar. Still in New York. Probably. Or near enough to see it.

Spinning around, she tried to open the window with her cuffed hands. It wouldn't budge. She turned around to study it and saw it was locked and nailed shut.

Great.

She looked around the room, hoping desperately that something had appeared out of nowhere and she could use it to break the glass of the window, but the room was as empty as when she'd first opened her eyes. She leaned her shoulder against the window, and it felt as solid as steel.

Trying to bust through with her body would *hurt*, and Kerry wasn't sure she could do it.

Boots stomped upstairs outside the room, and Kerry looked around for somewhere to hide. Impossible in an empty room. Swiftly, or as swiftly as she could with her feet chained together, she crossed back to where she'd woken up and sank back to the ground, trying to block out the smell of her vomit.

She didn't want her kidnapper to know she'd already kicked most of the drugs. She wasn't sure how her body would react to another dose.

The door opened and the kidnapper walked in. He made a dismissive sound when he saw her and hauled her up with one hand, half dragging her out of the room and across the hall.

She didn't have enough time to assess the situation, and any opportunity to escape disappeared in three steps.

She was off her game.

The kidnapper forced her onto a metal chair and hooked her handcuffs to one of the metal bars on the back of it. The chair was bolted to the ground. Should she take it as a compliment that he thought she needed so much restraint?

No. She really wished he thought she was weaker. She had no idea how to get out of this situation.

"It's time to talk, little girl." The kidnapper, who

she decided to just think of as Dick, had a raspy, threatening voice, and he sounded like he was enjoying this a little too much.

Kerry didn't say anything. Strangely, it was her witness training that kicked in. Dick hadn't asked her a question. She wasn't supposed to say anything.

He pulled up his own chair, identical to Kerry's except it wasn't bolted to the ground, and sat. He rested his hands on his knees and stared at her. It was too dim to make out his features clearly, but Kerry calmly met his eyes. If he was trying to intimidate her, it would take a while.

Her father would eat this man alive. So would she.

"What was in the package you were handing over on the night of the shooting?" he asked.

Shock ripped through her so quickly her mouth actually dropped open. "What?" The question popped out before she thought better of it. *That* was what he wanted to know? In a world of shifters and magic and shootings, he wanted to know the contents of a package from an art gallery? At least she could answer truthfully. "I don't know. Shouldn't your boss?"

He slapped her, and it was hard enough to wrench her head to the side.

Kerry winced as she looked back at him. But she

pushed aside the pain. Was it possible this man didn't work for AR? Was there another player in the game? She hoped not, because there would be no way Bryan could find her.

No. Bryan *would* find her. She just had to hold on long enough.

"The box disappeared before my employer could acquire it. Tell me what was in it and who has it, and I'll let you go." His hands were back on his knees, and though there was hate in his eyes, he was trying to sound civil.

Kerry wasn't buying it. He had no reason to release her, especially when she could call down the forces of proverbial hell to end him if she got free. "I never looked in the packages. I kind of assumed they were drugs. But I never even touched them. If your boss lost track of his delivery, that's not my fault." She probably shouldn't be answering, but she thought he was just warming her up. No one had cared about the package from that night until now, and there were better ways to ask.

"When my father hears you've taken me, he's going to raise hell. Let me go now, and you might make it out of this city alive." She didn't like relying on her dad for day to day problems, but this had something to do with him, and she wasn't above making him clean up his messes.

But was it possible AR Selby and her father were working together on this? Selby had shown up at her father's vacation home by invitation.

No. She and her dad had their issues, but he wouldn't give her up. But he wasn't the one looking for her either.

Would Bryan find her in time?

Worry plagued her right alongside doubt. She knew he'd look until there was no hope left, but it didn't mean he magically had the resources to do so. Would it even occur to him to ask her father for help?

No. Definitely not.

Shit.

She'd been gone for several hours, at least. At most a day and a half. She didn't think she'd been out for that long, though. She wasn't particularly hungry or thirsty. And apparently her system kicked drugs pretty fast.

Was a few hours long enough to find her?

There was a crash downstairs, and Dick whipped his head towards the door.

Maybe it was. Hope surged, and Kerry struggled against her bonds. They didn't budge. And her struggle was enough to bring Dick's attention back her way.

"Do you really think you're going to be rescued?" he taunted. "You're not getting yourself out of here."

He stalked towards her, violence in his eyes. Maybe there was an attack going down, maybe Bryan was going to rescue her. But Dick could do a lot of damage before Bryan found her.

This time he punched her, and it hurt so much worse than the slap. Kerry spat blood as her mind reeled, trying to figure out a way out of this situation. But every hit from his fists jolted her mind, and she couldn't focus.

Her vision was going fuzzy again, and it had nothing to do with the drugs.

She tasted blood in her mouth, and it was hard to swallow around her teeth. Her fangs. Her wolf was rising to the surface to defend her, and Kerry couldn't control it. This had never happened before and her mind reeled, trying to take control, even as she sank deep into her own consciousness to avoid the pain.

Then Dick leaned in too close and the wolf took her chance, lunging forward and tearing at his exposed skin until hot blood sprayed across her face. Dick's eyes went wide, and he clamped a hand on his throat. He stumbled back, even as blood poured out between his fingers.

He should have fallen. The wound should have been fatal.

But he somehow managed to get the door behind him open and stagger out of the room.

He wouldn't last long. And now that the door was open, Kerry heard the fighting going on in earnest. It sounded like a war zone down there.

Her body hurt every time she moved, but Kerry still struggled against her cuffs. Someone would come for her eventually, and if it was a foe, she needed to be ready. Her wolf had retreated deeper into her. But would shifting help?

The bonds were meant to hold human hands, her wolfish legs were smaller, and her claws would slide right out. But her position was all wrong. Wolf shoulders couldn't move like she was positioned.

If she tried to shift, there was a chance she completely screwed up her wolf's body and ended up even more injured than she already was.

Kerry had just decided to throw caution to the wind and try it when a shadow crossed the doorway.

Bryan.

Joy and relief washed over her as he rushed into the room. Then she growled when she saw that his cheek was bruised and bleeding. Someone had *dared* to lay hands on her mate? She'd make them pay.

She didn't know if that was wolf or woman talking, and she didn't care. No one got to hurt Bryan.

He knelt in front of her, hands not quite touching her, and she realized how bad she had to look. "Could be worse," she tried to say, but her lips were swollen and it was hard to talk.

Bryan made a sound in the back of his throat and took a deep breath before he spoke. Rage was loaded in every word, but it wasn't meant for her. "I'll kill him," he vowed.

She wasn't sure who he was talking about, but she didn't care.

He undid her bindings and helped her out of the chair. Already her wounds were starting to heal, but everything still *hurt*. They stumbled out of the room and into carnage. Blood stained the walls and the floor, but Kerry only saw two bodies.

No one was fighting as they picked their way through the room and out the back door, where a car was waiting.

A moment later, Gibson came sprinting out and yelled at them to start the car. They did, and the moment he was inside, Bryan put his foot on the gas and they sped away.

"Where's Jackson?" Bryan asked once they were on a highway and blending in with traffic. He kept checking his mirrors, most likely looking for a tail. Kerry hoped they weren't followed.

Gibson's tone was grim. "We had to split up. She knows what to do. I'm sure she'll find her way back to the warehouse."

But when they pulled in, she wasn't there.

# CHAPTER THIRTY

Bryan was putting distance between himself and Gibson. The major had spent the last hours pacing without letting up. The floor would give out before he did. Jackson still wasn't back, and they had no word she was okay.

And the longer time went on, the more likely that meant she wasn't.

Stasia and Owen returned shortly after he got Kerry settled into bed. She needed to sleep and heal. He wanted to wrap himself around her and promise her that all would be well.

But with Jackson gone, that might not be true.

Their intel had pointed to two likely places that Kerry might be kept. Stasia and Owen had taken the less likely of the two while he, Gibson, and Jackson hit their place. And it had been heavily defended. AR wanted to keep who he stole.

Had he stolen Jackson?

Stasia and Owen were in the kitchen, and though Bryan had avoided it for a while, he headed there to get away from the sound of Gibson's pacing. Would the man do that for any of them? Or was there something special about Jackson?

Stasia was digging into a salad as big as her head while Owen watched her in awe. "What?" she said around the lettuce in her mouth.

"You picked that instead of the pie in the fridge. How? This is a time of crisis. You need pie." He took a bite of his own piece of lemon merengue as if to prove his point.

"And when you're hungry again in half an hour, are you going to eat more pie?" She darted her fork out and snagged a bite of his pie for herself. Owen was fast enough to move the plate out of range, but he didn't even try.

"Obviously," Owen agreed. "I'll just keep eating it until I feel better."

She groaned. "You're terrible on a sugar high."

He grinned. "You love me."

Bryan had to make a noise before this got disgusting. "What was your location like?" He opened the fridge and was tempted to take a slice of the same pie that Owen was eating, but that would make Stasia glare at him. And, frankly, Stasia scared him a bit. He didn't want her judging him. He pulled out a premade sandwich and brought it to the table.

Owen had finished off his pie and was taking bites of Stasia's salad like he'd been invited. "Empty. We saw one security camera, but it wasn't functioning. The lock was child's play to bust. Nothing but a rat's nest inside."

Stasia shuddered. "I hate rats."

"Any word from Jackson?" Owen asked, his face uncharacteristically grim.

It had been nearly three hours since the op and she hadn't checked in. They all knew what that likely meant. The only question was whether she was captured or dead.

Owen's jaw firmed. "We haven't lost a member of our pack, and we're not about to start. We'll get her back."

Bryan hoped he was right. He ate half the sandwich and put the other half back in the fridge, appetite gone. He didn't want to interrupt Kerry's needed rest, but his wolf strained under his skin and demanded he go to her. She was his *mate* and she needed him.

Or perhaps he needed her. Maybe both were true.

He couldn't resist any longer.

She was in the process of sitting up when he entered, and she slumped back to the bed when she saw him. "I was coming to find you," she said.

"I'm here." Though it was dark in the room, he could see just fine. The damage from her capture had healed, at least physically. Her hair was a mess from laying down with it wet after the quick shower he'd insisted she take, but that was easy enough to fix.

"You're not close enough." She patted the bed beside her.

And Bryan was across the room in a blink, slipping off his shoes before he got under the covers. He would have taken everything else off too, but part of him was certain he'd be called out at any moment to go and rescue Jackson.

Or maybe that was just wishful thinking.

He gathered Kerry into his arms and finally felt something in him unclench. She'd been taken from him. Beaten. Held against her will. But she was here now and stronger than she'd ever been.

"How did you find me?" she asked. She ran a finger over a seam in his shirt, as if fascinated by the texture.

Those hours she'd been missing were the darkest of his life, and even with her safe in his arms, it was terrible to contemplate them. But she deserved to know. "First we got in touch with every police station we could to find out where they'd taken you. When that didn't pan out, we started searching traffic camera footage."

Her hand stopped and her eyes widened. "You can do that?"

"Jackson could. She's a bit of a tech wiz." And if one of them had been taken instead of her, then she would be scouring every technology available to find them. "But we only hit pay dirt when she went through the documents that Stasia and Owen grabbed from her brother. We found two properties that were good places to hold someone. Stasia and Owen hit one, Gibson, Jackson, and I hit the other. And we found you." It was a flimsy plan. None of them had been willing to say that out loud while they planned their assaults, but now the flimsiness of it threatened to crush him.

His hands started to shake, but Kerry wrapped her arms around him and held him close. "It's okay. You found me."

"I always will." Kerry owned his heart. Completely. His soul too, for that matter. It had happened so quickly and thoroughly that he belonged to her before he even realized he was falling. Now that he had her back, he had a chance to prove it. And he would. Every day. For the rest of their lives.

But he held those vows back. Maybe he'd wait until they'd known each other for two weeks to pledge his undying devotion. He didn't want to rush into anything.

Despite the horrible situation, he felt his lips pull into a smile. And though he'd been sure he wouldn't sleep, Kerry relaxed in his embrace and he followed not long after.

There was plenty wrong with the world. But he had his mate in his arms and he was ready to face it. With her.

One blink later, someone was pounding on their door, and a glance at the clock showed him he'd actually slept for six hours. He jolted up, while Kerry moved a bit slower.

Crossing the room in two strides, he jerked the door open and glared at Owen. "What? Any news on Jackson?"

"AR just filed a flight plan at a private airport. He's headed to Europe. But if we're fast, we can catch him before he takes off. Come on." Owen was already running back down the stairs.

And when Bryan turned around, Kerry was pulling on clothes of her own. "I'm coming with," she said before he could try and stop her.

Bryan pulled on his shoes and nodded. They didn't have time to waste, and she had the right to see this.

# CHAPTER THIRTY-ONE

Kerry knew this airport. Her father had flown in and out of it more than once. So had she, when she was a child. The rich and influential liked it more than using public airports, where they would have to interact with the masses.

Gibson drove them like the devil was chasing him. Apparently, he'd called in one of the millions of favors he was owed and managed to ground AR's plane for an hour due to a fake maintenance concern. But they'd needed almost all of that hour just to get to the airport.

Kerry had feared that they'd see Stasia's brother taking off just as they pulled in, but it didn't happen. And she wasn't sure how, but Gibson managed to get waved through straight onto the tarmac so they drove right up to AR's hangar.

He and his men milled around outside of the jet. These were business associates, not the same kind of people who'd kidnapped her. He was back in his businessman role today, no longer the man who could orchestrate a kidnapping and hire two dirty cops at the drop of a hat.

Her father would be so jealous if he ever realized what AR really was.

But they were lucky he was in his business persona today. It meant only his security guards were armed, and there were only two of them.

They piled out of their car and approached him. Bryan had almost said some nonsense about her waiting in the car, but he'd given it up after she glared.

Good. He could learn. That meant they had a future together.

One she was going to seize no matter what it took. The mark on her shoulder burned faintly, a reminder of all the things they could be to one another, if they tried. And she was going to try with all of her heart.

A woman with the demeanor of a powerful assistant marched up to them, the thin tablet in her hand her only weapon. She looked them over and her eyes locked on

Gibson, clocking him as their leader. Gibson was worse for wear today. Kerry didn't think he'd slept at all and his chin was covered in a day's worth of dark stubble mixed in with a small amount of gray.

"I'm sorry, sir, but Mr. Selby does not have any more appointments scheduled for this morning. Could you give me your name?" She spoke calmly, as if cars full of angry werewolves drove up to her boss every day.

Though she didn't know they were shifters.

Probably.

"Step aside," Gibson growled. His wolf had to be riding close for his voice to sound *that* feral.

The assistant gulped, but didn't give any ground. She was good.

"Let them pass, Gina," AR called out to them. "And give us space. This is a private matter."

The security guards turned to him with furious whispers, but by the time the five of them crossed the distance that separated them, the guards were off with the rest of the staff.

"That was brave, brother," Stasia said with raised brows. "Especially given the beating you deserve."

AR looked them over, but there was no fear in his eyes. Whatever was about to happen, AR thought he was still in control. "I never thought you'd become one of the monsters, Stasia. But I did need an in. I am sorry for using you."

Kerry didn't know what that was about, but it struck Stasia like a lightning bolt. "*You* were behind the kidnapping attempt? Why?"

He shrugged. "I needed to see Gibson's... pack... in action." He turned to Gibson. "I am sorry for betraying your trust. But I needed some way to track the project. You were a perfect candidate."

"You turned us into shifters? What possible reason could you have to do that?" Owen sputtered as the questions came.

"So you haven't figured that out. Good. Life needs some mystery." He stepped towards his plane.

Gibson stepped forward, and AR froze. "You're not leaving."

"I think you'll find I am." There was no fear in AR's voice.

Kerry stared at his hand and thought she saw something sparkle, almost like glitter. But AR was not a man to cover himself in glitter. Was his hand beginning to glow?

"The cops are on their way," Gibson lied.

And AR just smiled. "So they will arrest you for trespassing on a private airfield? My security guards are calling airport security now, and you *will* be taken into custody once they arrive. If you leave now, you might get away."

Fear whispered through Kerry. Being arrested once, even if it was a fake out, was more than enough for her. But Gibson didn't seem concerned. Or maybe he was too focused on his goal to care.

"Where's Jackson?" Gibson demanded. "Give her back and we'll let you go."

AR's brow furrowed, and the confusion looked real enough to Kerry. "Jackson?" he asked. He thought for a moment before nodding. "She's one of your shifters. The pretty blonde?" For some reason that made Gibson growl, but AR just shrugged. "I don't have her."

"Liar." Gibson was becoming more wild by the moment, the words barely intelligible. Kerry didn't know what would happen if he lost his grip on his humanity, and from the tension radiating out of the others, they didn't either.

"This game has gone on long enough. Walk away, Jericho. While you still can. Things are not as you think." He held up his hand, and it was definitely strange. Kerry wasn't sure if he was holding something glowing, or if it was his hand itself. It hurt to look at and she had to look away.

Gibson took a step towards him, and *that* made AR step back.

"Walk away, Jericho," AR repeated, and he held his glowing hand out like a talisman.

Gibson paused, grunted, and stepped forward again. Sweat poured down his forehead. AR was sweating too.

What the hell was going on?

The glow subsided and Gibson took three giant steps forward. He was only an arm length away from Selby. "What are you going to do now?" Gibson demanded, all traces of civility gone.

"Search my plane, if you must," AR relented. "We haven't even loaded the luggage yet." Then his voice got quieter—maybe he only meant for Gibson to hear. "Don't make this a bloodbath, Jer."

Gibson studied AR for several long moments before he held up a hand and signaled for them to walk forward. Owen and Stasia did, but Bryan put a hand on her shoulder to keep her in place. "He's less likely to hurt his sister," Bryan murmured.

That would have made sense in another world. But apparently AR had sent kidnappers after his own sister, which led to her getting changed into a shifter. And Kerry thought her family was bad.

Gibson stayed beside AR, tension radiating out of

every muscle. The man was ready to pounce, and a less disciplined man already would have. What was it costing him to keep from moving?

AR didn't pay any attention to Gibson, the threat dismissed. Instead, he studied her and Bryan. "Does your father know?" he asked. Then he smiled. "Of course not. I wonder how he'd react."

If it was a threat, it landed wide. While she'd been alone, she'd been worried about what her father might think, but she wasn't alone anymore. And why would her father believe AR? If he did, that was a problem for another day.

Several minutes later, Stasia and Owen stomped down the stairs of the airplane. "Nothing," Owen reported to Gibson. "She's not here."

"Where is she?" Gibson demanded.

Stasia stared at her brother. "Tell us and we'll go."

They'd have to go sooner rather than later. Kerry thought she heard sirens. But none of the others made a move back to the car, so she held her ground.

"Do you think I'm the only one involved in this little operation?" AR scoffed. "I don't have your friend. What use would I have for her?" He turned his gaze to Gibson. "I remember what you did. I've repaid your kindness with enough grief, I won't needlessly add to it."

Moral equivocating like that was how bad men slept at night. It made Kerry want to vomit.

Then AR looked at her. "As a show of good faith, I'll deal with your little problem. It seems some of my men have been freelancing. If I wanted you dead, you would be." He stepped back, and somehow there was a swarm of his people around him. "Now leave." His employees weren't completely between him and Gibson, but it would only take two steps for him to start using them as human shields.

And it would be a bloodbath. AR Selby wasn't maniacally evil—he wasn't laughing at their pain— but he had no qualms about letting others bleed for him.

Gibson knew it. And he relented.

They piled into the car, and AR headed for his plane.

Back on the road, Kerry barely breathed, waiting for the cops to find them. But the sirens she thought she'd heard never got close enough. When they were finally something approaching safe, some of the tension leached out of her shoulders.

"How can he control us?" Bryan asked. They were crushed together in the back seat with Owen. Stasia was smaller, but Owen had given her the front seat without a word.

"His hand glowed," Kerry added. "Or maybe he was holding something. I couldn't tell."

Gibson gripped the steering wheel tight enough she thought he might snap it. "Magic," he grit out. "We'll have to consult with the witches. This isn't the last time we're going to deal with AR Selby."

If Stasia had any concern for her brother, she said nothing.

The question still hung in the air. Where was Jackson?

And would they find her in time?

# CHAPTER THIRTY-TWO

THE SMELL of fish was overwhelming. It made Erin Jackson's stomach roil, and she had to swallow down her puke. Her clothes were already encrusted in blood. She didn't want to make things worse.

Her stomach roiled again.

No. Not her stomach. Her *everything*.

She cracked her eyes open, and for a second, thought she'd been blinded.

But, no, it was just dark. And her eyes adjusted quickly.

Metal. Low ceiling. Long, narrow room. And that incessant movement.

She was on a ship. Possibly out at sea. If that was true, it meant no one was coming for her.

Erin slumped even further in her seat, only her handcuffs and bound feet keeping her from sliding off.

She needed to find her own way out of this place, or she was a dead woman.

# CHAPTER THIRTY-THREE

Walking up to Michaels' office felt like some kind of fever dream. Kerry kept expecting *something* to go wrong. But no one tried to arrest her or shoot her. And she and Bryan hadn't even been bothered on the train.

Clearly something big had to go wrong.

But when she walked into the reception area of Michaels' office, the place was buzzing with energy, and she was led back to Michaels without a delay. Michaels had replaced the uncomfortable chair.

Huh.

Miracles did happen.

"I should have called you," the prosecutor said as she stood and greeted Kerry. "Things have happened very quickly this morning. It looks like you won't be testifying. The defendant has accepted a plea deal.

We're working out the documents to send to the court. Something could, technically, still fall through, but that's unlikely."

Kerry hadn't even sat down yet. "It's over?" She remembered what AR Selby had promised. Was *this* the "little problem" of hers that he was dealing with? "What made him change his mind?"

Michaels shrugged. "I couldn't say. Be on your guard for a little while longer while news of the plea deal trickles out. Harper is still looking into who attacked you, and we're not positive that the two things are connected. But if they are, hopefully your life is about to become much less interesting. I'm sorry for making you come all the way into town."

And that was her dismissal. Kerry headed back out to the reception area as if she were moving through a dream. Bryan was waiting and sprang out of his seat when he saw her.

"Is something wrong?" he asked. His eyes darted around, looking for threats.

Kerry smiled. "I don't have to testify. He took a plea deal. This thing is over."

Bryan grinned and wrapped his arms tightly around her. "That's great news."

The receptionist cleared her throat, and they split apart. "Let's get out of here," Kerry suggested. Hopefully she'd never need to darken the prosecutor's doorstep again. Once they were outside, she felt clear to talk again. "I think this was AR's work. The case was connected to him. I can't believe it's over." Her legs were a little wobbly as relief flooded through her.

She could go back to her normal life. As normal as it had ever been. Sure, she was still a shifter. And she'd somehow acquired a mate out of this whole thing. But there would be no more court case. Hopefully no more shootings. She could just be herself again.

Bryan led her to the edge of a little park where there was an open bench. He sat her down. "So when you say over..." He let it trail off, not quite asking a question.

She snapped her head his way. "You're not getting rid of me that easily." She grabbed his hand and laced their fingers together. "My wolf will take over right now and hunt you down." It was meant to be a playful threat. And it was.

Mostly.

But her wolf was primed just below her skin and waiting to hear how Bryan would react.

He kissed her.

Kerry let herself sink into it until a salacious whistle from somewhere down the street reminded her that they were *very* much in public. Reluctantly, she pulled back. "I'd invite you back to my place, but I think the door is still nailed shut." She hadn't had time to deal with the aftermath of the shooting and needed to get the repairs figured out.

But not today.

"Let me show you my place," Bryan offered.

"Yes."

His place turned out to be three train transfers away, but nearly an hour and a half on the subway later, they walked up to a surprisingly quaint building in Queens. There were planters hanging out of several of the windows, though late autumn meant that the flowers weren't in bloom.

Before she could make a comment, Bryan led her inside and up to the second floor. The apartment was bigger than hers and bright from windows shining light from two walls. It didn't look very lived in. There wasn't a spot of dirt on the floor, and the couch stared at a blank wall where a TV should have been.

"Do you actually live here, or did we break into a condo that's for sale?" she teased.

Bryan locked the door behind them. "I've been busy on jobs. I haven't spent much time here."

"Give me the tour."

He led her down the narrow hall and opened a door to reveal a bedroom that was dwarfed by the queen bed that took up most of the space. "Here's my room. Want to see the rest of the place?" He breathed the question into her ear.

Kerry shivered and kissed him.

The rest of the place could wait.

# EPILOGUE

Sweat poured down Jericho Gibson's forehead as he lifted the weight bar over his head for the seventieth time. He let the weights clank down and sat up, biting back a curse as his muscles protested.

He wanted to run up the stairs and demand progress on the investigation. Erin Jackson was out there somewhere, and they had to find her.

Under his skin, his wolf prowled. If he wasn't careful, the wolf would take over, and everyone would be sorry.

If she wasn't found soon, he'd let the wolf out himself.

Jericho stalked over to the punching bag and let go, fists flying in naked fury. The leather under his hands didn't give, didn't crack. But the bag swung and he stumbled, not expecting the motion.

He cursed.

She'd been taken four days ago and they had no leads. Nothing. And the trail was growing colder. Jericho knew what happened to missing persons cases that went cold.

Loved ones never got answers. And then they gave up hope.

But he *wasn't* giving up. Not today. Not ever.

He was going to find Erin Jackson.

And then his wolf was going to do exactly what it needed to do. She wasn't going to disappear again.

**Thank you for reading *Hungry for the Wolf*.**

## LOOKING FOR A LITTLE BIT MORE?

Sign up at the link below to **receive a free bonus scene featuring Bryan and Kerry** as they head out for date night and try their hands at some arcade games. Not so friendly wagers may ensue.
Link: https://katerudolph.net/hungrybonus

———

# Here's what you should read next:
## *The Alpha Heist*

**The alpha keeps what's his...**

No one steals from Luke Torres. His fortress is legend and his pack of lions are deadly, ready to face any threat. When Luke meets Mel, she knocks his socks off with a scorching kiss, but when they meet again, they are captor and captive in a deadly game of cat vs. cat.

**The thief is up to the task...**

From the moment Mel takes the assignment, she knows that it should be impossible. But for the supernatural world's foremost thief, impossible is an irresistible challenge. Especially when the payment for this job will get her one step closer to revenge. When the job goes belly up, she finds herself in the lion's den and facing off with the most alluring man she's ever met.

Can she find a way to complete the job without losing her heart?

# ALSO BY KATE RUDOLPH

**Guarded by the Shifter**

**Werewolf. Bodyguard. Mate.**
The origins of these shifters are shrouded in mystery,
but they're determined to protect their mates from
any harm that comes their way.
***Also available in audio!***
*Hunting Season*
*On the Prowl*
*Stalking Magic*
*Wolf Cursed*
*Hungry for the Wolf*

———

**Stealing the Alpha**


**The thief takes what she wants, but the alpha keeps what's his...**

Join shifter thief Mel as she clashes with lion alpha Luke in an explosive trilogy of two opposites who can't keep away from one another.
***Also available in audio!***
*The Alpha Heist*
*Entangled with the Thief*
*In the Alpha's Bed*

———


**Alien Mates: Planet Exile**


Guerran is no place for pretty human women. But these alien heroes will protect their mates!
**Also available in audio!**


Exile's Hunter
Exile's Adored

———


**Zulir Warrior Mates**

**Kidnapped humans. Alien Warriors. Electric wings.**

The Zulir Warrior Mates series brings you human heroines and heroes abducted from Earth who find love – and wings! – with the alien warriors who rescue them.

***Also available in audio!***

*Synnr's Saint*

*Synnr's Hope*

*Synnr's Spark*

*Synnr's Kiss*

———

**Dragon Brides**

**Dragon Princes. Fierce Women. Love.**

Fated mates, fierce women, and dragon princes are ready to find their mates.

*Crux*

*Ranger*

*Saber*

*Cipher*

*Storm*

*Drake*

---

**Mated to the Alien**

**Fated Mate Alien Romance**

Detyens are doomed to die young if they don't find their fated mates.

Follow along as these mated pairs fight off aliens, corrupt dictators, prejudiced humans, pirates, and more! The books can be read or listened to in any order, though some characters show up in multiple stories.

***Select books available in audio.***

Pick a book and jump into the action today!

*Ruwen*

*Tyral*

*Stoan*

*Cyborg*

*Krayter*

*Kayleb*

*Shayn*

*Braxtyn*

*Doryan*

*Dekon*

---

## Detyen Warriors

**Detya was destroyed a hundred years ago. These doomed warriors are out to find justice... and their mates.**

The Detyen Warriors series brings you kick butt heroines, alpha alien heroes, fated mates, and relationships strong enough to span the galaxy!

**The entire series is also available in audio!**

*Soulless*

*Ruthless*

*Heartless*

*Faultless*

*Endless*

———

## Alien Holiday Romance

Christmas... in space????

These alien holiday romances look beyond Earth's winter holidays and ring in the season across the galaxy!

***Select titles available in audio.***

*Snowed in with the Alien Beast*

*The Alien's Winter Gift*

*The Alien Reindeer's Wild Ride*
*Trapped with her Alien Mate*

———

## Alien Outlaws

**Outlaws, schemes, and love... it's all there in the Alien Outlaws series...**

Andie Munster is sick of life on Ixilta, the planet she got dumped on after being abducted from Earth six years ago. And when the mysterious and dangerous Xandr shows up looking for a way off the planet, she's half-prisoner, half-co-conspirator in a wild rush to escape.

*Rogue Alien's Escape*
*Rogue Alien's Woman*
*Rogue Alien's Secret*
*Rogue Alien's Legacy*

———

**Find more by Kate Rudolph at** www.katerudolph.net

# ABOUT KATE RUDOLPH

KATE RUDOLPH IS paranormal and sci-fi romance writer who lives in Indiana. She loves writing about kick butt heroines and the steamy heroes who love them. She's been devouring romance novels since she was too young to be reading them and had to hide her books so no one would take them away. She couldn't imagine a better job in this world than writing romances and sharing them with her fellow readers.

If you enjoyed this story, please consider leaving a review.

www.ingramcontent.com/pod-product-compliance
Lightning Source LLC
Chambersburg PA
CBHW061533210726
48287CB00006B/1935